Disclaimer

enrichment of storytelling and the exploration of human nature across imagined borders.

Foreword

There is something enduring in the human impulse to uncover what is hidden — to search for the truth buried beneath appearances. In every story within this collection, a crime has occurred, yes — but more than that, a veil has been drawn. These are not tales of blood, but of shadows.

Some of these mysteries unfold in familiar cities; others, in quiet places *where silence lingers longer than truth. The detectives, like the readers, are not always certain, not always right. But they are seekers — and it is the act of seeking that defines the heart of each tale.*

These stories were written not to tie every thread neatly, but to stir something — a shiver, a realization, a question. You may solve the mystery. Or you may find, as I often do, that the mystery solves something in you.

STORY 1: THE MONACO AFFAIR

Once a native of Prague, Kristina Havelková—now known by her married name, Kristina Blanc—had recently lost her husband. Newly widowed, she inherited a vast fortune and, in the wake of her grief, resolved to begin anew in the principality of Monaco.

She was but thirty-five years old—a splendid age to start afresh. With her russet-blond hair, vivid green eyes, and a figure full and well-proportioned, Kristina was a woman of notable allure.

Wherever she went, she attracted admiring glances, and it took her little effort to make a lasting impression upon the bourgeois circles so accustomed to the company of celebrities.

Upon arriving in Monaco, Kristina purchased an apartment in the most fashionable of districts, within the opulent Tour Odeon Double Tower, a gleaming edifice completed in 2015 and designed by the celebrated architect Alexandre Giraldi. Her apartment, located on the seventh floor, offered every comfort. The building boasted a twenty-four-hour concierge service and, on its lower levels, an array of amenities: housekeeping, valet and limousine services, an indoor pool, a business center, a private cinema, a gourmet supermarket, and the renowned Odeon Café. This splendid residence rose proudly in the La Rousse–Saint Roman district, the highest of Monaco's residential elevations.

The staff of the high-rise were impeccably trained, their appearance and demeanor beyond reproach. They ensured the utmost in service and discretion for all who lived or visited there.

Kristina promptly hired an interior design specialist to furnish her home. She had no desire to clutter her new space with trinkets. What she sought was cleanliness and comfort—no more, no less. New furniture was ordered from catalogs, and in due time, the apartment took on a refined and harmonious character. Everything was fresh, modern, and welcoming.

On the walls hung tasteful lithographs by celebrated artists. Here was Andy Warhol, with his iconic digital portrayal of Marilyn Monroe; there, a sumptuous Renoir painting of a full-bodied nude reclining languidly on a settee. A third piece—a striking portrait of the English queen—was the work of the modern artist Lucian Freud, grandson of the famed psychoanalyst Sigmund Freud. Each of these artworks was formally listed as a lithograph in documents notarized by the local legal authority.

The early days of autumn arrived. After the swelter of a Mediterranean summer, a welcome coolness stirred the air. Kristina's new life was unfolding with remarkable grace and ease. And so, on this, the first Sunday of September, she prepared to attend a Sunday brunch. She selected a form-fitting navy-blue dress with a plunging neckline, swept her hair into a tidy chignon, and dusted her face, neck, and décolletage with a silken powder. Around her neck, she clasped a pendant from Van Cleef & Arpels, a golden piece wrought from shaded gold and malachite. She surveyed herself in the mirror, assessing her finest features: her striking green eyes, the gently waved hair of a warm caramel hue, her flawless complexion, and her full, expressive lips.

From her wardrobe, she took a vivid red handbag of crocodile leather adorned with a gold skull-shaped clasp set with diamond-studded eyes—a bold creation by Alexander McQueen. Spritzing her neck and wrists with her favorite scent by Creed, she descended into the lobby, where a valet in uniform greeted her with a smile and handed her the keys to her Mercedes.

She started the engine and drove along the broad boulevard to the Hotel Hermitage, where Sunday brunch was held each week in an atmosphere of luxury and leisure.

As she entered the lobby, Kristina found the space pleasantly quiet. She made her way into the dining hall, where the brunch was underway. The buffet abounded with a dazzling variety of fare, and waiters—mostly men—moved deftly between tables, bearing large trays and offering delicate, gourmet portions on porcelain plates small enough to fit in one's palm.

As Kristina perused the offerings, a man in a maître d's uniform approached her. Middle-aged and wearing a polished smile of porcelain perfection, he introduced himself as Jacques Dubois. "Pardon, madame. May I ask your name?"

"Kristina," she replied with a smile.

Jacques proved effortlessly charming. In short order, he returned with a bottle of Dom Pérignon Brut Champagne, vintage 2006. They toasted and drank on a shared promise. Thus began a light, unburdened conversation. Jacques made a striking first impression: a man of stature, with silver at his temples, a trim haircut, and a face of symmetrical elegance. Fluent in French (his native tongue), German (from his ancestry), and English (acquired in childhood), he moved with ease among Monaco's elite. He seemed to know all the regulars and was welcomed among them as one of their own.

The air was light with music, laughter, and the refined scent of culinary delights—the very elixir of a charmed existence. And so, amidst this graceful atmosphere, Jacques and Kristina became acquainted, learning just a little about each other.

Jacques was unmarried and moved in a wide circle of acquaintances, both male and female. Kristina, new to these aristocratic ranks, was still unfamiliar with their unspoken rules—despite the considerable fortune now at her command.

Soon—too soon, perhaps—Kristina, without hesitation, invited Jacques to her apartment. And thus began a casual romance, unbound by promises...

The first time Jacques Dubois stepped into Kristina's apartment, he couldn't help but feel a twinge of envy. The artworks of world-renowned painters, the understated elegance of the furnishings, the spaciousness devoid of ostentation—it all spoke of cultivated wealth. The soft beige leather of the sofa in the salon invited repose. Kristina and he sat side by side and ordered dinner from the Odeon Café, delivered promptly to their door.

For starters, they were brought fresh burrata and bresaola, arranged delicately over a bed of greens. Jacques chose veal liver, seared over high flame, while Kristina was served sea bass baked in foil with roasted potatoes. For dessert, there was a luscious house-made tiramisu accompanied by two steaming cups of cappuccino.

They barely touched the salad or the burrata. The cappuccino they finished with ease, savoring a spoonful or two of the ethereal tiramisus. Then, Kristina turned on some music, and together they began to dance—slowly, closely, as if the room itself had grown smaller around them.

Jacques Dubois was a seasoned seducer. Yet in his presence, Kristina felt safe, cocooned in a sense of charm and familiarity. When they had first met, she had asked him plainly, "Can I trust you?"

Jacques had answered with a solemn nod.

They spoke mostly in French, switching to English on occasion, when needed. He had shared a little about himself, and Kristina, though charmed, only knew the broad strokes of his life.

Jacques had long moved in elite circles, surrounded by the nobility of Monaco. This association was his greatest credential. Yet, as with many men of polished surfaces, he kept certain truths locked behind a gentleman's smile.

First, Jacques harbored affections for both women and men—though he never spoke of this in detail. Second, and more pressingly, he had lost a great deal of money in gambling halls across the Riviera. His debts had grown monstrous, their weight pressing on him each waking hour. All that remained in his possession was a small apartment in Nice, and the shadow of a debt that would not cease growing.

He knew he was walking a razor's edge.

And then came Kristina.

She had captivated him—genuinely—and he watched her with keen interest. What he hoped for was a relationship unbound by obligation, one that would let him slip away at any moment, unburdened and unseen. Still, it wounded him to see the idle lives of his acquaintances—aristocrats in the fifth generation—wasting both their time and others'.

Though Jacques relied on their approval, he harbored contempt for the haughtiness of their world.

That was why he liked Kristina. With her, everything felt easy.

But had she known the full truth about him—his vices, his debts, the tangled knots of his dual life—she would never have agreed to meet him alone in her home.

One early autumn day, they took a drive together through the scenic surroundings of Monte Carlo. Along the way, they stopped at a quaint bistro for lunch. The fare was traditional: duck with mashed potatoes and a green salad, followed by cappuccino and dainty chocolate éclairs.

They sampled each dish but left most untouched. The coffee, however, they drank to the last drop.

Afterwards, Jacques suggested they return to Kristina's apartment. The mood was light, and as they drove down the wide highway in companionable silence, music played softly, and each was lost in their own thoughts.

Once home, Jacques offered to pour a little more wine. Kristina, by then exhausted, could barely stand. She slipped into her bedroom, removed her dress, and donned a sheer blue peignoir. Then she approached the heavy safe in the wall, keyed in her secret code, and the door creaked open.

Kristina took off her earrings, her pendant, her rings, and a thick gold bracelet, placing them carefully inside. Then she locked the safe once more.

Moments later, Jacques appeared with two glasses of champagne. Kristina took a small sip, swayed to the bed, lay down—and almost immediately slipped into sleep. She did not move.

Jacques did not touch her. Instead, he turned to the safe. He keyed in the code—quietly memorized earlier while watching her open it. The door opened once again.

He glanced back at Kristina. She lay motionless. Her breathing was soft.

"Good," he whispered. "I have time."

Swiftly, Jacques began removing the contents: bundles of euro and dollar bills, velvet boxes filled with gold and platinum jewelry, encrusted with diamonds and precious-colored stones. All of it went into a large, zippered Louis Vuitton duffel.

Once the safe was emptied, he shut it carefully, zipped the bag, and crept softly to the door.

He turned the handle with utmost care, slipped out into the corridor, and descended the building's emergency stairwell, used in cases of fire. He was barefoot, his steps light and urgent.

Outside, he darted through a tunnel toward the main highway, then walked briskly to a taxi stand. Along the way, he pulled on a dark cap, slipped on black sunglasses, and changed into a pair of Adidas trainers.

"There," he murmured. "No one will recognize me now."

At the stand, he slipped into the second taxi in line and requested a ride to Italy. The driver, a young foreigner who spoke poor French, nodded and took him as far as northern Italy.

Jacques paid in cash and continued on foot, across the border…

In a small provincial town in Northern Italy, Jacques purchased a wig of silvery-gray hair and a thick matching beard. He checked into a modest hotel and, in the privacy of the bathroom, affixed the wig and carefully glued on the beard. The transformation was dramatic, altering his appearance almost completely.

Soon after, he hailed another taxi, this time instructing the driver to take him through the Alpine tunnel into Austria. With his mastery of three languages—French, German, and English—Jacques navigated the journey with relative ease. He paid exclusively in euro notes, a precaution born of long practice.

He had now been on the run for two days.

On the third, weary beyond measure, he resolved to reach Munich, nestled on the Bavarian side of the Alps. In a small mountain inn, he paid for a room and requested a bottle of water. Once alone, he peeled off the wig, detached the beard, and sank into a deep, dreamless sleep.

On the other end, back in the principality of Monaco, Kristina Blanc awoke early that morning. Stretching languidly, she glanced about the apartment. It was empty. Jacques, it seemed, had left for work without saying goodbye.

"Well, so be it," she murmured with a shrug.

She wandered into the kitchen, placed a slice of bread into the toaster, and laid a wedge of cheese atop the warm, crisp surface. "Such delicious bread," she thought as she stepped onto the balcony to admire the morning vista.

Birds chattered cheerfully in the trees, and the soft hum of the city drifted up to the seventh floor. The Mediterranean light glimmered on the horizon.

After a warm shower, she dressed in her new light frock and approached the safe. Calmly, she entered the secret code. The heavy door swung open.

She reached in—then froze.

Her chest tightened as panic flared within. This could not be. Jacques Dubois was a man of impeccable standing in high society.

She stood motionless, as if carved in alabaster.

Then, slowly, as the shock began to lift, Kristina picked up the phone and called the police.

"I've been robbed," she said, trembling. "The safe in my apartment —it's been emptied of all its contents."

Her accent thickened with distress, and her words tumbled out in disarray, but the officer on the line was patient and attentive. Within ten minutes, the Monaco police arrived.

Kristina recounted all that had happened. At last, with steely clarity, she declared the name of her suspected thief: "Jacques Dubois." The officer's eyebrows rose in disbelief.

"Pardon, madam. Could you repeat that name?"

"Jacques Dubois!" she snapped, her voice now cold with fury. The officer fell silent.

"Forgive us, Madam Blanc," he said gravely. "But we must search your entire apartment. May I inspect the paintings as well?" Kristina nodded, still visibly shaken.

The officer approached the portrait by Lucian Freud, carefully lifted it from the wall, and began to examine it closely. Saying nothing, he inspected the frame, the canvas, the backing.

Then, gently, he turned to Kristina and, in a tone both professional and kind, said, "We would like to take several of the artworks for expert examination. If they prove of significant value, you may wish to present them at a Sotheby's or Christie's auction. I can promise nothing yet, but it may be worthwhile."

The Monaco police launched a Europe-wide alert. Word spread swiftly across borders. Within hours, photographs of Jacques Dubois were circulated to customs agencies, border patrols, and investigative bureaus in Austria, Germany, Italy, and beyond. From the sleek corridors of Interpol to the provincial police stations of alpine towns, the manhunt began.

But before dawn broke, the sound of forceful knocking and raised voices shattered the quiet.

"Monsieur Jacques Dubois, you are under arrest! You are charged with the theft of valuables from Kristina Blanc of Monte Carlo!"

The local German police, acting on instructions from the investigative unit in the Principality of Monaco, had tracked him down. They burst into the room, handcuffed him as he sat dazed on the bed, his face drawn and aged by stress and sleepless nights. "Monsieur Jacques Dubois, you are hereby ordered to surrender all stolen property belonging to Kristina Blanc, with whom you were recently acquainted!"

Jacques was too stunned to speak. In his mind, he whispered a farewell to Kristina, and a half-hearted plea for forgiveness—from her, from fate, from whatever god might still be listening.

He'd planned it all—Mexico first, then a flight to Belize, and after that, nothing but silence and sun-drenched freedom.

But in that decisive moment, when he opened Kristina's safe, he had not thought of customs officers. Nor had he considered the watchful eyes of European border patrols.

He never stood a chance of reaching Mexico.

Two days later, as dawn broke once more, Kristina fetched the morning papers from her doorstep. There, staring back at her, was Jacques Dubois—arrested in Munich, hair wild, his face twisted in terror.

In his Louis Vuitton duffel bag, authorities had recovered all the valuables: the jewels, the cash, the heirlooms—untouched, intact.

That very day, the Monaco police contacted Kristina. Jacques Dubois had been apprehended, and by the next day, she could reclaim the bag containing her stolen possessions. Meanwhile, the paintings Kristina had inherited from her late husband had undergone meticulous authentication. Beneath each modern lithograph, hidden behind layers of canvas and clever framing, the experts discovered a second image—a secret artwork. These clandestine masterpieces, painted in oil on small wooden panels, were by none other than the Flemish masters: Jan van Eyck, Pieter Bruegel, and Peter Paul Rubens.

At Kristina's request, the paintings were submitted to Sotheby's for auction.

The sale brought in a fortune.

With newfound means and unshaken elegance, Kristina Blank invested her wealth in properties across her beloved cities—in Belgium, in France, and in her native Prague.

Revenge was never her aim. But dignity, restored, was its own exquisite justice.

STORY 2: THE BLOODY RUBY OF MONTREAL

The city of Montreal looked like something out of a snow globe in mid-December.
Snow glittered like shards of crushed glass, coating the streets, trees, and buildings.
Fresh drifts piled high against lampposts and along storefronts. Shoppers moved
slowly along the avenues, bundled in thick scarves and fur-lined coats, their breath
clouding the icy air.

The cold had teeth that day—the kind that gnawed into your bones, sharp and
unrelenting. The wind whistled in piercing gusts, flinging snow in

dizzying spirals.

Pedestrians shuffled along, heads bowed against the storm, while store windows

twinkled with holiday displays.

Henri Montaigne had seen many cold cities before, but there was something

about Montreal that bit harder than most. It wasn't just the wind. It was the

people, the strangers, the way faces disappeared behind scarves and frost-covered

glasses. His eyes scanned the streets with the focus of a man used to being

watched. Not all strangers were strangers, after all.

He wore a sleek black coat, and a gray cashmere scarf tucked neatly at his throat. In

his right hand, he clutched a leather briefcase secured to his wrist by a metal cuff.

It was no ordinary briefcase, and Henri was no ordinary man. The metal clasp on his wrist dug into his skin as the wind fought to tear the briefcase from his grasp. But he held tight. Always tight. Always ready.

Henri Montaigne was born into a family of craftsmen. His father repaired watches

in a small workshop in Lyon, and for years, it was assumed that Henri would follow

the same path. But it was his uncle Jules who changed everything. Jules had a side

business in gemstones—uncut diamonds, sapphires, and rubies—and his workshop

was a wonderland of glinting treasures for young Henri.

"Look at this," Jules once said, holding a raw emerald up to the sun. "In its raw

state, it's just a rock. But carve it right, and it's a king's ransom."

Henri had watched his uncle polish the stone, rubbing it with steady patience until the surface gleamed like a forest at dusk. It was magic. From that day on, Henri's world expanded. By his early twenties, he was working for international gem traders, traveling to Antwerp, Jaipur, and Madagascar.

Only recently, Henri had returned to Madagascar. The air there was unlike anything he had ever known—thick with heat, and the stench of diesel clung to skin and cloth alike. On one of these overseas trips, Henri was introduced to a gemstone dealer named Kofi.

This time, he wasn't looking for sapphires or garnets. He was hunting something rarer. Above all, he prized one stone—a gem that burned with deep, vivid crimson—a rare ruby with a story behind it. Kofi, a man from southern Africa, knew such stones well.

The ruby is one of the most precious of jewels. Large rubies are rarer than diamonds of equal size. The largest gem-quality ruby ever found weighed 400 carats and was discovered in Burma.
In the East, the ruby was especially revered. Eastern cultures believed in the stone's mystical power: to stir the soul toward greatness, to warn of danger through a change in hue, to shield its bearer from lesser spirits, from malevolence, from enchantments.

Henri met Kofi in the back of a narrow market stall, past rows of men selling fruit,
coffee, and counterfeit watches. Kofi was lean as a whip, with sharp eyes that
didn't blink. When he pulled out the blood ruby, the world stopped for a second.

"It's yours," Kofi said, smiling a little too wide. "But know this, Monsieur
Montaigne. It's already taken blood, and it will take more."
"Superstitions," Henri scoffed. He paid Kofi with crisp American dollars and
tucked the ruby deep into his briefcase.
As he walked away, he glanced over his shoulder. Kofi was still watching him—eyes narrowed, lips curling into a smile Henri would never forget.

Henri made swift arrangements and left for Canada on the first available flight, lingering no more than a few hours. He travelled lightly; his most treasured possession did not weigh much. After changing flights in London and Toronto, he finally reached his destination: Montreal.

Passing through customs was effortless. He smiled benevolently as he was cleared without questioning. Once outside, he made quick arrangements for a limousine.
Inside the comfort of the vehicle, he gave the driver an address and dozed off as the car sped along the deserted highway from Pierre Elliott Trudeau International Airport into downtown Montreal.

Within the hour, he reached the Sofitel Hotel, the city's most exclusive luxury destination, where a doorman in a red coat tipped his hat and swung open the grand revolving door.
"Welcome back, Monsieur Montaigne."

Henri nodded and stepped inside, checked in, and took an elevator to his customarily assigned suite.

After retreating into the room, he punched in the code for the safe and placed the case inside.

Henri changed his clothes for a black cashmere sweater and dark gray pants

that had a relaxed fit. He felt light and breathed easy with the precious ruby in the
safe of the most prestigious hotel.

Henri took his wallet, slipped it into his inner pocket, and went downstairs to the bar
that was open until a late hour. It took him just a few minutes, and he was in the oblong room with dimmed lights, with Paul Mauriat playing softly, "Love is Blue." He sat on a tall chair by the bar counter and eyed the room: "Whisky on the rocks, please!" he said in his husky,
tired voice.

The bartender handed him a drink. He turned around to check his surroundings and sighed with relief. The music was soothing and romantic and struck a chord deep within him.

The next moment, he felt somebody patting him on the back. He was startled and looked around
Henri faced a woman, slightly drunk, with cheeks flushed from alcohol and bright red lipstick.
The woman licked her lips and asked, "Would you like to spend some time with me?"
Henri grimaced and said firmly, "No," then turned away—and then, on the spur of the moment, he stood up, briskly left the bar and took the elevator to his floor.

It was getting dark outside, with a strong wind howling, composing a tune of its own. His inner voice was telling him not to leave the hotel, but he had to meet another gemstone dealer from Antwerp that night. The arrangement had been made weeks earlier.

"Okay, I'll go," Henri told himself.

He moved like an automaton, gripped by a sense of foreboding. He was careful by nature, but even for him, things occasionally slipped beyond control. Henri opened the safe, took out the case, and hooked it to his left hand. He was tense, his nerves drawn tight like a coiled spring. He walked to the elevator, feeling the oppressive hush of danger settling around him. Henri pressed the call button, stepped inside when the doors parted, and descended smoothly to the ground floor.

Henri stepped out, looked around, and felt certain no one was following him. It was indeed getting darker, although the streetlights were bright enough to illuminate the snow-covered streets. A strong wind pierced through his coat. Henri shivered and walked with determination. The alleyway was darker still, with only a few lanterns lighting his path along the sidewalk, where the snow drifted like silvery dust on velvet. He walked with purpose toward his destination.

At the turn of the alleyway, he felt their presence. Henri sensed them before he saw them. The man in the gray scarf. The blonde woman with frost-bitten cheeks. The man in the flat cap. They were never too close. Never too far. But they were there. Always.

He quickened his pace, clutching his coat tighter. His breath fogged in front of
him in sharp, frantic bursts. Snow crunched underfoot, and every step echoed
far too loudly in his ears. His eyes darted to the left. The blonde woman. Same coat. Same
hungry stare.

He cut down a narrow street, ducked into an alley, pressed his back against a wall.
His pulse thudded. His breath came out in gasps. Footsteps.

"He's close," said a voice—a woman's voice. Sharp. Confident.

Henri pushed off the wall, sprinted out of the alley, and made for the crowded

boulevard. Although it was relatively late, pedestrians were still walking with

shopping bags toward their destinations. He pushed through them, scanning the

crowd. No sign of them.

A breath of relief.
Then—

"There he is!"

Henri didn't think. He ran. His boots slipped on patches of ice. He cut across the

street, nearly getting hit by a taxi. The horn blared, but Henri didn't turn back. His

chest burned. His lungs begged for air. He darted down another alley, weaving

through trash bins, his pulse drumming in his ears.

Footsteps behind him. Louder now. Closer. The flat-cap man was fast. Too fast.
Henri could hear him breathing.

He dashed into a corner café, panting, heart rattling like a drum.
He crouched behind a table, eyes on the door. The bell above the entrance jangled.

The blonde woman walked in. She scanned the room slowly. Carefully.
Her eyes passed right over him. Then they locked.
Her lips curled into a grin.

"Hello, Henri," she whispered.

He bolted out the back exit. Henri reached an open lot. His breath fogged the air like smoke.

No cover. No escape.

The three of them circled him like wolves.

"Drop the case, Montaigne," Flat cap growled.

"The ruby, Henri," said the blonde woman, tilting her head like a bird watching prey. "Don't make this ugly."

Henri's fingers tightened around the case, which was still firmly sealed to his wrist by a metal clasp. He could feel it—the warmth, the thrum, the weight of it.

He raised the briefcase over his head, eyes wild with defiance, forgetting that he had never locked it with the magic key. A thought struck him, scalding hot.

"Come take it," he hissed, grimacing in sharp pain.

Flat cap lunged. They collided. Henri hit the ground hard, his back slamming against the ice. The breath flew from him in a hot rush, and when he opened his eyes, the blonde woman was there, crouched beside him, her breath misting in the cold.

Her hand gripped the ruby. It pulsed once, like a heartbeat. His eyes widened.

Goddamn it. He forgot to close the case, his final thought throbbed through his mind as the steel clasp dug into his wrist. He thought of revenge, fury burning behind his eyes, and with his last breath, he tightened his grip on the case.

Henri coughed once. Blood spattered the snow. It looked like the ruby—red on white. A perfect gem.

The blonde woman tilted her head, the gem in her palm. She gazed at the ruby with reverence. Her lips curled into a smile.

"They'll remember you, Henri," she whispered, cradling the gem like a newborn. "But only for the blood you left behind."

Henri Montaigne was buried in a snow-blanketed cemetery outside Montreal. No mourners. No epitaph. Only the wind whispered his name — and the ruby he died for vanished into silence. It passed from one careless hand to another...

In the weeks that followed, the city moved on. The snow melted. Headlines faded. The case, like so many, slipped into silence. Henri Montaigne became a name without a face, a man buried beneath frost and forgetfulness. And as Montreal thawed, so too did the trail of those who had vanished into the night—untouched, untraced, and unspoken of. Until, half a year later, they surfaced once more...

Six months slipped by like smoke through a keyhole, and now, at last, spring had returned. The streets, once scoured by wind and blanketed in frost, began to stir with life anew. Buds pushed their way through the thawed earth, and pale green leaves unfurled like whispered promises. The air no longer bit—it hummed, soft and damp with the scent of rain and soil. The city, once glazed in silence and snow, blinked awake beneath a gentler sky.

The three had disappeared swiftly with their loot and reappeared half a year later, in late April, in the same café where the meeting with the intermediary, Kofi, had taken place.
Celestia, Oro, and Niku — the one in the flat cap — had long belonged to a syndicate of colored gemstone hunters, fencing their spoils in Amsterdam through a web of trusted intermediaries.

Celestia was the youngest among them. She was but twenty-five. Her figure was all bones and skin, gaunt and sharp-edged. Her eyes were coal-black, her hair naturally the same, though dyed a glaring blonde, with dark roots ever showing. Celestia's wardrobe changed as her purpose did.

She was a killer — feared even by her comrades. She had no past, and so, it seemed to her, no future either. She did not know her true date of birth. Her adoptive parents once told her she might have been born in spring, somewhere in Greece — though even they were uncertain. Celestia had fled that family long ago and joined Oro and Niku not long after.

Following the murder of Henri and the capture of the blood-red corundum, the trio did not flee far — merely across the border into France, to Paris, to sell the plunder. They sold it all: watches, jewelry, even narcotics.

The money was laundered through small jewelry shops scattered across Europe.

They arrived in Paris in the early morning, traveling by train and changing lines along the way. Spring had just begun to stir. Celestia wore a long black skirt, flared and blooming with great, vivid flowers. Her sweater was warm and dark. Over her shoulders, she had draped a silk scarf patterned with red roses.

Throughout the journey, she fingered her prayer beads and muttered a rhythmic whisper under her breath.
A great resentment coiled within her — toward the steady, conservative world, where children lived with parents in tidy homes. It was envy laid bare — a bitter jealousy of bourgeois comfort and respectable peace.

Oro and Niku were not far removed from Celestia. Like her, they claimed to be children of the streets, as they always liked to say. In truth, they had never truly studied anywhere, yet they could drive well and handle a smartphone with surprising ease.

Upon their arrival in France, they already knew who the buyer would be.
He was the owner of a modest jewelry shop — an aging Frenchman, discreet and precise. Though fully aware that the ruby was stolen, his

fascination with rare stones eclipsed both fear and morality. He had to possess that singular gem.

So, Kofi had told him — Kofi, who claimed to know everything and everyone.

Oro and Niku warned Celestia that they would be meeting with a wealthy jeweler, and she would need to dress accordingly: a tailored pantsuit and heels.

Celestia was quietly furious but said nothing. She followed the others into a ready-to-wear boutique.
There were hardly any customers inside. It was the end of the workday, and the shop stood empty. It would close in an hour — at eight in the evening.

Celestia stepped into the shop and gasped. Silk chiffon blouses hung before her like delicate clouds.
She knew nothing of fashion, but these were Armani — and she liked them at once.
She asked the saleswoman to show her two: one a deep emerald green, the other a dark navy adorned with tiny flowers.

Celestia entered the fitting room. A suit and the two blouses were brought to her.
She changed swiftly into a pinstriped navy suit and the green blouse, pinned up her hair, and stepped out to meet Oro and Niku. They both gasped.

She looked like an entirely different woman.

She asked for a pair of black leather heels, and when she emerged from the boutique and walked down the broad central street, passersby turned their heads — caught by the strange enchantment of Celestia in such conservative attire.

Niku and Oro followed her into a small café and took seats at the back, where they awaited Monsieur Louis Vernon.

The café was dim and nearly empty. A waiter approached, leaving paper cups and a bottle of mineral water on their table.

Almost at once, Monsieur Louis Vernon entered, glanced around, and spotted the trio seated in the shadows. He approached.

"Bonjour, madame et messieurs!" greeted Louis Vernon with genteel flair.

Celestia studied him closely. For the first time in her life, she offered a slight, approving smile — and nodded.

Without a word, Niku reached into his inner pocket and drew out the ruby, wrapped in a plain napkin. He placed it upon a square of black velvet.

The precious stone shimmered with brilliant light, and it seemed to all present that tiny crimson rays spread from its heart.

They sat in silence, staring at the gem's otherworldly beauty. Then Niku spoke.

"I'm from Kofi," he said. "He told us the stone was found in Burma and brought to Antwerp."

Monsieur Louis Vernon examined the ruby in silence.

The others watched. No one spoke a word.

At last, Vernon asked, "Name your price."

A pause followed.

None of them knew much about pricing or the intricate workings of the gemstone market.

Niku muttered, barely audibly, "Ten million euros."

Louis Vernon said nothing.

He wrote a check for the amount, took the stone gently, placed it in a velvet box, and tucked it into his inner coat pocket.

He rose, nodded farewell, and swiftly exited the café.
Down the street he walked, entered a Mercedes, and started the engine.

Then he felt it — a presence. He turned quickly.

Celestia was in the back seat, staring ahead, her eyes burning with rage.

"Hand over the stone," she said softly. "It's best if you do it without a struggle.
Otherwise, you won't make it to your destination. I'll kill you here and now."

She drew a small black pistol fitted with a silencer.
Monsieur Louis Vernon, an aristocrat of the fifth generation, turned to her calmly.

"It would not be wise to kill me here in Paris. The gendarmes are everywhere. You'd be caught, and in the end, they'd execute you. Wouldn't it be better if I sold you something beautiful instead — a brooch, earrings, a necklace — whatever caught your fancy? Then you could learn a trade, find a job, marry, live a life."

Louis Vernon had the look of a wealthy patron from an old cinema reel. He could tell at once: Celestia was, to put it kindly, of little intellect and immense bitterness toward the world.
She gnashed her teeth, but something held her back. She offered something strange.

"Fine," she said. "I'll come to your shop. You'll gift me something."
Monsieur Vernon nodded.
"Agreed."

Celestia, who had not the slightest understanding of the value of fine jewelry — nor even a bank account to her name — smiled faintly.

Only Niku held the money, under his name alone. The others — they were but hands in the operation.

Monsieur Louis Vernon, as if playing roulette, could have driven straight to the gendarmerie and handed Celestia over.

But instead, for reasons known only to him, he brought her to his jewelry shop. There, he walked in and triggered the alarm with a hidden switch.
Within a minute or two, the sirens of police vehicles howled in the streets.
The silver-haired Monsieur Vernon smiled, revealing his flawless porcelain teeth.

Celestia stood motionless. There was nowhere to run.

Not far off, parked on the street, sat a car. Inside were the two bandits — Niku and Oro — pistols drawn, ready to fire.

Celestia didn't resist. She simply stared at the display cases — glittering rings, pendants, tiaras — all so close, and yet forever out of reach.
As the gendarmes burst through the door, shouting commands, she remained perfectly still, the pistol slipping from her hand like a discarded toy.

Outside, Oro and Niku fled the scene in a panic, tires screeching against the cobblestones. They would vanish into the shadows for now — but shadows do not protect forever.

And as for the ruby — the blood ruby — it was locked once more in the vault beneath Monsieur Vernon's shop.

But he never wore it. Never sold it. Some say he feared its curse. Others say he admired it too much.

Either way, it sat in silence, pulsing faintly in the dark — a stone that had seen death, carried vengeance, and whispered to its bearers the price of their desires.

A ruby not born of love but sealed in blood.

STORY 3: THE GOLDEN PRAGUE

Golden Prague, in the waning days of August, was an especially enchanting city. The leaves atop the trees had begun to yellow, while the grass in the parks remained a vibrant green, dotted with budding violets and daisies. Trams emitted melodic trills as Prague's residents strolled and relaxed in the parks, seated on large wooden benches, reading books and newspapers, **or** sharing news with friends. Grandmothers sat with prams, knitting new garments for their grandchildren.

Two young women, Irma Kudelka and Katrina Repka, had journeyed from a neighboring town to Prague to wander the city, browse the shops, and visit their favorite bistro to indulge in juicy sausages with mustard, washed down with dark beer. But first, they stopped by a local internet café to "surf the internet," an activity always both useful and interesting. Unexpectedly, they stumbled upon a dating website featuring foreigners. There were numerous profiles accompanied by photographs—Germans, Frenchmen, Italians, and even a few rather pleasant-looking men from North Africa. The profiles detailed the virtues of the candidates, who were professionals: doctors, engineers, bankers, and generally wealthy individuals. However, it must be said, as indicated in the descriptions, they were all between forty and fifty years old. Irma and Katrina gasped in admiration, covering their mouths with their hands as they examined the early-greying and slightly airbrushed men in the photographs.

Simultaneously, they decided, "Let's send them selfies with our photos." The girls photographed each other and immediately uploaded the pictures to the dating site. Within literally a minute, they received a notification that they had been recognized as the most beautiful women in Europe. Irma and Katrina had never doubted this. Irma, a blonde with blue eyes, and Katrina, a brunette with green eyes, both practiced rhythmic gymnastics and, in terms of physique, had no equals.

Pleased with themselves, the girls headed toward the center, closer to Charles Bridge, and entered a local bistro to have coffee and, if they had enough money, to order at least one apple strudel with vanilla ice cream. They sat at a table by the window and ordered dessert and a glass of light semi-sweet wine. After a short rest, Irma was the first to speak, expressing her dislike for the dating site.

"It's some kind of pirate site, and there could be unexpected unpleasant surprises. What we need is to look for a good job in the Arab Emirates. They say the pay is good, and if we go there together, it will be more fun."

The girls opened the necessary website and saw an advertisement offering a secretarial office job in Dubai.

"Well, this is just great," exclaimed Irma. "I think we can earn good money there, and upon returning, we'll still have time to rest and go to Bulgaria by the Black Sea."

Without much deliberation, they sent their résumés via email, indicating knowledge of three languages and attaching their passport photographs. Exactly five minutes later, they received a response stating that if they were ready for an interview with company representatives, the firm would pay for a one-way ticket to the Arab Emirates.

The girls agreed, and a few days later, they boarded a Lufthansa plane in Prague with a layover in Frankfurt on Main. They took only the essentials, packed into a small travel bag. The plane was filled with people from various countries, all seemingly returning home to the Arab Emirates. The women were dressed in abayas, covering almost their entire faces, which was unusual for Irma and Katrina, who wore simple silk-colored jumpsuits and white tank tops. Their hair was secured with clips, and they wore dark glasses. The men on the plane, many of them, were dressed simply in trousers and T-shirts, with almost all sporting thick, jet-black beards.

Irma and Katrina observed the people on the plane with interest. Living in the Czech Republic, they had never seen representatives of the Arab world. The only thing that came to both their minds were tales featuring a sorcerer, a magician, a wizard in a turban with a bag from which the head of a snake emerged—its mouth hissing open, red tongue extended and glistening like a blade.

A stewardess approached, bearing glasses of tea and small packets of nuts along with a slice of apple pie. The girls drank the strong tea and gazed out of the porthole, watching clouds drift by.

After a few hours, they landed in Frankfurt. The airport, as always, teemed with people—a colorful crowd of tourists with large bags adorned in bright patterns, brimming to the top. The girls wandered the main hall before heading toward their gate for the connecting Lufthansa flight.

There was already a long queue at the boarding gate, and once again they observed the same scene: men dressed in flowing white garments with head coverings held in place by black bands, and women entirely concealed in abayas, some even with their eyes veiled by translucent cloth.

They boarded the plane to Dubai, which taxied across the tarmac, then gained speed and rose into the air. Irma and Katrina were not frequent fliers; more often, they journeyed across Europe by train. But in that moment of ascent, their hearts fluttered joyfully, and they looked out as Frankfurt grew smaller and smaller, until it vanished completely from view.

They tried to distract themselves by watching films in French, but a steward soon approached and politely asked, in German, that they refrain from watching foreign films and suggested instead the Al Jazeera news channel. The girls grew uneasy. Where would they live? Where would they work? With whom would they make friends? They had not considered these questions.

As a kind of forewarning, a bearded man in traditional white robes and a head covering approached their row. With a frown and a sharp gesture, he curtly ordered them to switch off the television. The girls exchanged a glance, startled but silent, and did as he said. As he walked away, they leaned toward each other and whispered —not curses, but angry remarks in Czech— an anxious protest shared between frightened hearts.

The plane landed safely the next day in the Arab city of Dubai. After passing through customs and a narrow, dimly lit corridor, they were met in the arrivals hall by a bearded man holding a sign printed in English:

"Warm Welcome to Irma Kudelka and Katrina Repka in Dubai."
"Well, this is nice," Irma thought, as the two girls exchanged glances. The man spoke poor English and was difficult to understand, but the girls showed him their Czech passports. He almost smiled.
They extended their hands to greet him, but he turned away without a word and strode toward the exit. The girls quickly followed. A black Mercedes stood waiting just outside the terminal. The man never properly introduced himself, but he muttered something vaguely resembling a name.
They climbed into the back seat, and the car sped along a wide highway. After half an hour, they arrived at a modest building. The man used a keycard to open the door, and they stepped into what looked like the lobby of a small hotel, though they weren't certain. Then, with a sudden turn, the man spoke in Russian—but with an accent: "Passports, please. Registration. My name is Ibrahim." The girls nearly said, "Nice to meet you," but the words caught in their throats. Silently, they handed over their passports. Ibrahim turned toward the elevator and gestured for them to enter. They obeyed, now deeply unsettled.
The man led them through a hotel-like corridor to the last door. He swiped his keycard; a green light lit up. He opened the door without a word, then gestured again for them to go in. Even if the girls had wished to run, they wouldn't have known how to escape the building.
They realized—this man was a criminal, perhaps armed. For now, they must comply. This was a trap. They were without passports. Irma's heart sank. Katrina laid a hand on her chest and whispered a prayer: "God, help us." At least Irma's grandmother and Katrina's

mother knew nothing. They were safe in the Czech countryside—
Irma's grandmother with the family children by the Vltava River,
and Katrina's mother, a company clerk, working on silk exports
from Uzbekistan to Italy for the great Armani's exclusive line.
Ibrahim paused, then added, "You'll dance at a strip club for
foreigners. Tomorrow at seven in the evening, I'll collect you for the
night show."

The girls turned pale but said nothing. Ibrahim continued, "Food is
in the fridge. In the morning and evening, you'll be brought meals—
hot breakfast, dinner at night. Fruits and water are in the fridge.
That's all. Here are your robes." He tossed something black and
heavy on the floor—it was an abaya.

"When you leave the room, wear the abaya over the bikini." He laid
sealed bundles of evening outfits on the table. Then, without a
farewell, he turned and left.

The girls exhaled in relief. Irma whispered, "Now we must figure
out how to escape." They opened the fridge: grapes, melon,
watermelon, dates, and various cold dishes.

"Well, at least we won't starve."

Irma said aloud with a touch of irony, "So, we're dancing a
striptease." They examined the costumes Ibrahim had provided:
glittering panties and bras adorned with rhinestones and Swarovski
crystals.

"I have an idea," said Irma. "We'll wear these over our flesh-colored
gymnastic bodysuits."

She retrieved a unique, form-fitting leotard that covered the whole
body. "We'll put the decorative pieces over this."

The girls spent a sleepless night in the silent hotel, with not a sound
drifting in from outside. In the morning, they took a shower and
glanced out the window. There, not far from their own, was a
balcony—close enough to leap to, perhaps—but again the question

arose: how and where would they run?

"We must wait and see what happens next," whispered Irma, pressing her hand to her mouth. Katrina added at once, "We need to find the police and ask to be taken to any Western embassy."

The entire day they drifted about the room, stretching and training as if at a ballet barre. They gripped the backs of chairs.

"We'll perform the routine we used at the European gymnastics tournament in Paris," Katrina said. "You'll see—someone in the audience will surely approach us, perhaps offer money. And perhaps that person will speak a language we know—German, maybe, or English. We'll ask for help."

That evening, they applied makeup, twisted their hair into tight buns like athletes before competition, and prepared as if for a final performance.

At the appointed hour, Ibrahim arrived. He wore a proper suit and white shirt, though he looked sinister—his long, black beard lending him a menacing appearance. Again, he offered no greeting, only gestured for them to follow. He handed them black abayas and veils. Dressed in ballet slippers and veiled from head to toe, they followed him silently to the car.

As the vehicle sped along the broad, empty highway, the girls felt their athletic instincts spark—despite the fear, their bodies moved with the familiar rhythm of warm-up stretches.

The car arrived at a towering skyscraper. They stepped out and followed Ibrahim to the main entrance, where a doorman stood—a man dark as pitch in ornate livery, smiling with a row of flawless white teeth. He seemed African. Seeing their pale faces, he offered a warm nod. Ibrahim handed over some bills, showed a card, and the doorman allowed them entry.

They rode the elevator to the thirtieth floor. The doors opened onto a luxurious space: a grand restaurant hall where a pianist played a melancholy Eastern melody.

Ibrahim motioned to a side door. Inside the small dressing room, the girls threw off their abayas and head coverings, revealing flesh-toned leotards. Over them, they donned the glittering bras and panties encrusted with rhinestones and Swarovski gems. They powdered their faces and painted their lips a bright, cheerful shade.

Then the door opened. They stepped into the hall, smiling and swaying their hips as they walked through the room, blowing kisses to the audience. The music, soft and unobtrusive, played in the background. They began their performance—elegant, acrobatic, a graceful echo of the routine that had once earned them gold in Paris. The room fell silent. All eyes turned to the two performers. Few had seen gymnasts of such caliber—almost acrobats, their movements refined by rigorous ballet training.

When the dance ended, applause erupted. A man from the front table —clearly a European, clean-shaven, dressed in grey slacks and a white shirt—leapt to his feet and whispered to Irma:

"I'm from the German embassy. I'll help you. Where are you from?"

"Czech Republic," Irma answered quickly.

"We'll meet tomorrow. Same time, same place. Agreed?" He glanced at both girls. As he spoke, he discreetly tossed euro bills onto the floor and pressed money into Irma's hand.

But at that moment, he noticed Ibrahim approaching. The man quickly stepped away and returned to his table, pretending nothing had happened.

"Who was that?" Ibrahim asked sternly.

"He offered me money," Irma replied without blinking. "Why, I don't know—maybe for the beautiful dance." She smiled, pleased that Ibrahim did not understand foreign languages.

Ibrahim remained silent during the drive back, scowling at the wheel. The girls also kept silent, watching the roadside, trying to memorize the route to the hotel.

When they arrived, it was completely dark outside—no streetlights, not a glimmer. Ibrahim turned on the flashlight on his smartphone and shone it ahead for the girls. They entered the building. The elevator rose, and Ibrahim unlocked their door. Without a word, he shut it behind them.

They exhaled, pulled milk from the fridge, drank a glass each, and ate flatbread with cheese. Everything was edible, but their hands trembled from fear. Katrina began to cry.

Irma gave her a stern look and whispered, "Tomorrow we escape. After the performance." Katrina shuddered and walked to the window. The street was deserted.

But beyond their view, a new thread of hope was already forming.

What the girls did not know was that someone had already taken notice. Seated in the shadows of the club was a man who had not applauded—only watched. Henri Graf, a diplomatic attaché with the German consulate, had been tracking suspicious reports involving Eastern European women arriving in Dubai under vague employment contracts. When Irma and Katrina took the stage, he leaned forward ever so slightly. Their posture, their poise— something about them didn't match the usual dancers he'd seen while gathering intelligence in similar places. He made no move that night, only slipped out a side exit before the applause ended. But he returned the next day—with a plan.

They barely slept that night, drifting into exhausted slumber only near dawn. When they awoke, they silently washed, drank coffee, and began to stretch.

"Plié. Battement. Stretch into the splits. Keep your back straight," commanded Irma. "We must pretend everything is fine. We need our strength for tonight. Nerves of steel. No giving in."

That evening, precisely on time, Ibrahim entered their room. His tone was sharper than ever as he barked, "Put on the abayas. Tonight, you will dance—and this time, remove the bras and panties."

Irma's mind raced. Thank God, she thought, that no one—not even Ibrahim—had noticed the flesh-toned bodysuits beneath their glittering costumes. The fabric was opaque and durable, designed specifically for ballet dancers—impossible to tear without scissors. It was their secret armor. Wrapped once more in black veils and cloaks, they stepped into the waiting car. It sped along the silent highway, the desert sprawling around them in an endless hush. And again, the question pulsed in their minds: How would they escape this gilded prison?

The car pulled up in front of the familiar skyscraper. The same doorman awaited, his dark skin glowing under the lantern light. Ibrahim slipped him some cash. With a practiced nod, the man opened the door.

The girls took the elevator to the thirtieth floor. They moved down the hall to the side room, quickly undressed, revealing the bodysuits still hidden beneath their clothes, and put on the fresh glittering lingerie—this set even more ostentatious than the last. They powdered their faces, painted their lips a deep, vivid red, and inhaled slowly.

The door opened. They stepped once more into the lion's den.

This time, they entered with a flourish, blowing kisses to the audience, hips swaying with deliberate, polished elegance. The music started—a mournful melody that faded too quickly. But the girls needed no guide. They moved to their own rhythm, their steps fluid, synchronized, mesmerizing.

As the performance reached its climax, they tore away the glittering costumes, revealing the skin-toned leotards beneath. For a beat, the hall fell into stunned silence—then erupted in thunderous applause.

Through the throng, the man from the German embassy appeared. They recognized him at once. As Henri Graft approached, he dropped euro notes to the floor, stepped closer, and whispered:

"Don't be afraid. Follow me. Your captor's been locked in a restroom. While the applause continues, come with me."

The girls bowed in unison, as they had done so many times before. Then, with swift determination, they followed the man. He led them to the express elevator, handed them new abayas, and guided them through a hidden exit, where a black Mercedes waited.

"Lie down flat," Henri ordered in English. They obeyed at once, hearts pounding, limbs curled into tight bundles of silent resolve as their savior climbed into the driver's seat.

"You are safe now," he said softly, glancing back. "I am a representative of the German consulate in Dubai. You're in good hands. Soon, we'll switch vehicles. We're heading toward the border with Oman. I hold a diplomatic passport. They won't search me."

He fell silent, focusing on the road.

Meanwhile, Ibrahim lay bound and gagged in the club's restroom, his thoughts dark and spiraling. He couldn't call for help—he was in the Emirates illegally. Worse still, the girls' passports were tucked into the inner pocket of his suit jacket. He couldn't go to the police. He couldn't even scream. The black Mercedes raced through the night toward a narrow escape. The diplomat—tall, composed, and steady—kept his eyes fixed on the dusky horizon as the car sped toward the border.

"We're nearing a checkpoint," he murmured. "Soon, you'll need to hide in the trunk. The border guards may ask questions. But I have a diplomatic passport. That gives us a chance."

The car rolled to a halt along a desolate stretch of road. The sky above Oman was tinged with twilight. The diplomat stepped out, stretched his limbs, and opened the boot.

"Quickly now," he said gently. "Lie flat. We won't be long."

The girls, clutching their borrowed courage, climbed in, curled tightly like frightened swans, and whispered, "God protect us." He closed the trunk with care.

Moments later, the vehicle approached the border. Customs officials stepped forward. One, a man in a white dishdasha and a golden headdress, approached the driver's side.

"Passport," he demanded.

The diplomat presented it: Henri Graf, emissary of the German Consulate.

A glance. A nod. Permission granted.

The car eased forward into Oman.

Once they were safely out of sight, Henri pulled over. He opened the trunk, and the pale faces of Irma and Katrina blinked up at the blinding morning sun.

"We've made it," he said, quiet triumph in his voice. "Now, let us rest."

They found a humble roadside shop. The girls washed their faces, drank water, and donned once again the abayas Henri had given them. Then they returned to the car, now seated like passengers, not fugitives. In their hands were fresh German travel documents bearing their names: Irma Kudelka and Katrina Repka.

"Thank God," Katrina whispered.

They reached the airport in Muscat. After freshening up, they waited in the lounge until their flight was called. Soon, they would be bound for Istanbul. Henri approached once more. He handed them tissues and small bottles of water.

"This is the final leg," he said warmly. "From Istanbul, you'll fly home—to Prague."

Meanwhile, Ibrahim lay in the dim, solitary confines of the club's restroom, wrists bound, mouth sealed with tape. He could scarcely move, and his thoughts grew wild and desperate.

"I can't report this," he thought grimly. "I'm in the Emirates illegally. The girls' passports are in my coat pocket. If someone finds them—"

He squirmed and writhed, trying to make noise, to bang or shout through the gag, but his strength was waning. At last, after what felt like hours, the door opened.

A man in a hotel staff uniform stepped in, surprised. He quickly cut the cords and peeled the tape from Ibrahim's mouth. Ibrahim tried to speak, but his voice cracked.

The man asked something, and Ibrahim muttered in Russian.

Suddenly, the hotel worker responded in the same language—but not kindly. He swore, cursed, barked his words like slaps. Ibrahim blinked, stunned.

"You're Tajik?" the man asked gruffly.

"Yes," Ibrahim admitted, and with that, he sprang from the restroom, bolted down a side stairwell, and escaped through a service exit. It took him half an hour, breathless and muttering curses, to reach the street.

"Damn Europeans!" he spat. "I brought them girls, and this is how they repay me?"

He hailed a taxi and rushed back to the apartment where the girls had been kept. The place was completely deserted.

Panic began to bloom. *"I must disappear before I'm tied to a scandal,"* he thought grimly.

An hour later, Ibrahim reached the airport. He purchased a ticket to Oman and from there planned to travel to Istanbul—for food, for pleasure, and then to vanish back to his mountain village in Tajikistan.

Onboard the flight, he sat in the rear, avoiding attention, not eating or drinking, staring out the window like a man watching his life unravel.

When the plane began its descent, a flicker of hope stirred in his chest—but it was not to last.

As the aircraft descended smoothly into Istanbul, Ibrahim's thoughts were full of grilled kebabs, strong tea, and the comfort of a temporary hideaway. His stomach growled; he hadn't eaten in hours. He imagined the bustling streets, the smoky scent of spices, and the cool anonymity of a rented room.

The wheels touched down softly.

Then—a voice over the intercom:

"Remain seated. Security personnel will be boarding momentarily."

The cabin grew hushed. The door opened. A group of men in dark uniforms entered, bearing the emblem of Interpol. They moved swiftly, silently, like shadows with authority.

They marched down the aisle.

Passengers turned in their seats. Whispers erupted. Necks craned.

The Interpol officers stopped at the last row.

"Ibrahim?"

The man barely had time to look up before cold steel closed around his wrists.

The officers did not speak again. They escorted him down the aisle, a pale, sweating figure with lowered head and unkempt hair, flanked by justice. Cameras flashed. Bystanders stared. Some clapped. Others merely watched.

Outside, the officers placed him in a waiting Interpol vehicle, its black frame gleaming beneath the airport lights.

The car rolled through the winding roads of Istanbul toward the city's central police station. No music played. No one spoke. Ibrahim murmured incoherently, cursing fate, foreigners, and his own poor luck. But it was over.

The trap had sprung.

And thus, the tale came full circle — a web of deception, desire, and deliverance.

Irma and Katrina returned to Prague not as girls, but as women forged by fire — silent witnesses to a world they had never imagined, survivors of a darkness they refused to let define them. The streets of Golden Prague welcomed them with the gentle rustle of leaves and the warmth of familiar sun. And though the scars remained, so too did the steel in their spines. For sometimes, the fiercest strength is found in escape — and the bravest victory, in coming home.

STORY 4: THE GALACTIC SOCIETY
Meeting on the Extraterrestrial Meridian

Paris on Christmas Eve shimmered with all its splendor. The air was crisp, and soft, fluffy snowflakes floated gracefully over the city, disappearing the moment they kissed the cobblestones. The festive streets pulsed with life as Parisians and visitors strolled through the Christmas markets, sipping mulled wine spiced with cinnamon and savoring golden, freshly baked pies filled with sweet preserves. There was an air of quiet hope — a belief that on such enchanted nights, miracles were possible.

Beyond the city, perched on the outskirts, a medieval castle rose from the wintry landscape. Its gray stone walls loomed like the bastion of an ancient fortress. This was the Papal Palace of Avignon, one of the most monumental Gothic structures in Europe. Tonight, it was not kings, cardinals, or popes who gathered there, but the members of the secretive *Our Galaxy Club*, an assembly of the world's foremost scientists, parapsychologists, engineers, and dreamers, all united by one profound purpose — the search for extraterrestrial life.

Fifty select members had been invited from around the world. Each one, a seeker of the unknown, had arrived from distant lands to participate in this grand symposium. The Papal Palace, once the seat of Western Christianity, had become a temple of cosmic inquiry. Invitations had been sent to renowned astrophysicists, astronomers, mystics, and explorers, and now they filled the great hall with their presence. It was an annual tradition, but this year, something was different.

A grand feast awaited them in the central hall, where the glow of flickering candlelight cast long, golden shadows on the ancient stone walls. A banquet fit for royalty had been prepared. The long oak table, draped in an emerald-green cloth, was adorned with Christmas garlands of holly, red berries, and golden bells. The centerpiece was a roasted pig with crisp, crackling skin, surrounded by hearth-roasted duck glazed with honey, and platters of fish arranged in intricate patterns. Fresh salads, cold cuts, and pyramid-shaped towers of fruit punctuated the spread. Between the dishes, bottles of thirty-year-aged red wine and Dom Pérignon champagne stood like sentinels. Silver platters held meat pies fresh from the oven, their golden crusts still glowing with warmth.

At the head of the table sat the club's leadership, their faces bathed in candlelight. Each of them was as unique as the constellations in the night sky:

- Dr. Leandro Silva, the Brazilian president of the society, was a man of quiet presence. Tall and lean, his bald head shone beneath the light of the chandeliers. His black sweater and loose-fitting trousers gave him an air of detachment, as if he observed the world from afar.

- Dr. Aisha Faruq, the vice president from Pakistan, was a bold, brilliant aerospace engineer. Her wild, curly hair framed a face of sharp intelligence. She wore practical trousers and lace-up boots, eschewing elegance for function, and her sharp eyes watched every movement in the room.

- Sophie Duval, the secretary from France, was a woman of poise and precision. Her hair, a chestnut brown chignon, framed her face with elegance. She wore a finely tailored dress and a Hermès scarf tied playfully around her neck. Her sculpted figure, encircled by a Louis Vuitton leather belt, made her the unspoken icon of elegance at the gathering.

- Omar Al-Farisi, the Emirati treasurer, was a man of wealth and wisdom. His beard was streaked with silver, and he wore a pristine white robe with a perfectly arranged keffiyeh. His commanding presence filled the room as he watched over the assembly like a vigilant falcon.

- Dr. Yumi Nakamura, a radio astronomer from Japan, was a man of silence and calculation. With a slender frame and analytical eyes, he observed every moment with precision. His tuxedo was as crisp and meticulous as his thought process.

- Professor Samuel Okoro, the Nigerian anthropologist and mythologist, wore a colorful kaftan and a small cap. His deep voice carried the authority of ancient wisdom, and his insights into celestial myths had captivated the club for years.

- Dr. Ingrid Bauer, the German propulsion engineer, had a soldier's pragmatism. Her hair was cut short like a soldier's, and she wore a simple, sleek black jumpsuit. Her grey eyes scanned the room with the precision of a watchmaker, always seeking flaws in design or logic.

- Alejandro Torres, the parapsychologist from Argentina, was a man of mystery. His appearance was never the same. Sometimes he wore wigs, sometimes beards, and other times he arrived bald and clean-shaven. Tonight, he wore a sharp black tuxedo and his natural hair, and he moved with the smooth grace of a cat.

The evening began with a toast. Luca Romano, the Italian master of public relations, stood at the head of the table, his Armani suit immaculate. With his charismatic smile and magnetic presence, he raised a glass of Dom Pérignon.

"To the extraterrestrial meridian," he declared. "To the stars. And to Mars."

Glasses clinked. Laughter filled the room. Plates were passed, and conversations unfolded like constellations forming in the night sky.

As the feast continued, the topics grew deeper. They discussed UFO sightings, theories of time machines, and the possibility of building a permanent human base on the Moon.

Dr. Ingrid Bauer explained her proposal for a Perpetual Motion Engine, which would revolutionize space travel. She spoke of time dilation, referencing Einstein's theories.

"If we are to travel to Mars and beyond," she declared, "we must master the control of time itself. Imagine it: a time machine, not to go backward, but to control the flow of time during interplanetary journeys."

Alejandro Torres smirked. "Time is not an object to be controlled," he said, leaning back in his chair. "Time is a shadow, and shadows cannot be grasped."

"You're wrong," said Dr. Yumi Nakamura. "We are bound by time, but physics tells us it can be stretched, bent, or even halted. With the right conditions, time is no longer a river but a sea we can navigate."

Later that night, Luca Romano announced a shocking update. He read a police report regarding Orionne Lumira, a club member who had gone missing. The room fell silent. The police had found him unconscious on a bench by the Seine River in Paris. He had been assaulted, his suitcase stolen. His hands bore defensive wounds, as if he had fought off an attacker.

"Lumira told police," Luca announced, "that he was carrying fragments from the 1947 Roswell UFO crash — evidence he intended to gift to the club."

Whispers swept through the hall. If this was true, someone had stolen more than a suitcase. They had stolen proof of extraterrestrial life.

The next morning, they gathered for elections. Alejandro Torres was unexpectedly chosen as the new chairman. He laughed, claiming, "I hypnotized you all to vote for me." The crowd half-laughed, half-grumbled, and later chose Sophie Duval as president, with Dr. Yumi Nakamura as vice president.

On New Year's Eve, the club celebrated one last grand dinner. Ingrid Bauer wore a midnight blue gown sparkling with Swarovski crystals. Alejandro Torres wore a tuxedo, his eyes glinting with humor. At midnight, knights in medieval armor strode into the hall carrying ornate gift boxes. Each member received a gift — a gold bracelet engraved with a secret message:

"To the seeker of truth. May your path lead you to the stars."

The clock struck twelve. Champagne flowed, and music echoed through the ancient halls. Samuel Okoro raised his glass and declared:

"Brothers and sisters, tonight, we journey beyond the stars."

The night ended with laughter, music, and the clinking of glasses. As dawn approached, a private coach took them to Charles de Gaulle Airport. One by one, they parted ways, each headed to distant cities.

But before they boarded, Sophie Duval raised her glass one last time.

"To the stars," she said softly.

The others echoed her words.

"To the stars."

And somewhere beyond the distant clouds, the stars watched.

The Habsburg Castle Assembly

Spring had arrived. Sticky green leaves had begun to unfurl on the trees, and the air was filled with the scent of grass and blooming flowers.

Late in the evening, the members of *Our Galaxy Club* arrived in Vienna, the capital of Austria. Spirits were high, and even after their long journey, they chose to wander the city — famed for its splendor.

At the Vienna State Opera and Ballet Theater, a grand festival was underway. The entire city was adorned like a stage set. Above the streets, whimsical sculptures of people hung in the air, while in the central park, benches were occupied by papier-mâché figures of Viennese citizens. Banners were strung from lampposts, and by nightfall, the city center was awash in a symphony of colored lights.

The following morning, the members boarded a train that would carry them through the mountains into Switzerland, to a small town where stood the ancestral castle of the Habsburg dynasty, built in the eleventh century.

The organizers had chosen this location precisely because it was remote — inaccessible to ordinary tourists. Their purpose: to examine all known incidents of unidentified flying objects in near-Earth space, and to hear reports on so-called portals — places believed to be arrival and departure points for unknown aerial phenomena.

The Habsburg Castle, a medieval fortress in the canton of Aargau on the banks of the Aar River, was the birthplace of one of Europe's most powerful dynasties. Until 1415, the House of Habsburg had resided there, and from this stronghold had risen an empire that would one day shape much of the Western world.

By nightfall, the society members reached the canton of Aargau and took shelter at a small riverside inn. The tavern's keeper, an elderly Frenchman, welcomed them and invited them to supper.

Inside, guests sat at long, rough-hewn wooden benches arranged around heavy rectangular tables. The tavern keeper, assisted by his young daughter — a blue-eyed blonde — brought out deep steaming bowls of meat stew, accompanied by thick slices of rye bread. The travelers ate heartily, then climbed the stairs to the rooms above, laid down upon straw mats, pulled woolen blankets over their shoulders, and drifted into a deep, dreamless sleep.

Come morning, the guests descended to the ground floor to find a modest surprise awaiting them. Wicker baskets brimmed with warm morning pastries — sweet buns filled with jam and wild berries. In the corner stood a coffeepot, with tea, juices, and yogurt set nearby.

At the table, conversation turned lively as they discussed recent developments and shared whispers of sightings.

After breakfast, they made their way to the hall where the meetings were set to begin.

This time, the assembly was presided over by Sophie Duval, the poised and eloquent president of the Society, and Luca Romano, the famously elegant Italian journalist and author.

Among those gathered were names spoken of with reverence — not for their titles, but for their tireless devotion to the unknown.

- Celestia Arcanum, a theoretical physicist, brought fresh research on particles smaller than atoms — their nature still cloaked in cosmic secrecy.

- Orionne Lumira, now recovered from the violent Paris incident, returned with new insight and unshaken resolve.

- Dr. Stella Varis, the chemist, continued her study of asteroid matter fallen to Earth.

- Astrid Vortex detailed strange physiological effects in animals returned from space.

- Dr. Seren Elara tracked the lingering impact of cosmic radiation on the human body.

- Cosmina Veyra, the mathematical physicist, analyzed planetary data across the galaxy.

- Zara Nocturna decoded distant signals from the void.

Others — Nova Eldryn, Lyra Eclipsa, and Vespera Aether — were researchers from the Loma Linda laboratories, seeking signs of life on newly discovered worlds.

Their findings were regularly published in *Our Galaxy*, the society's monthly journal — a treasury of scientific articles, speculative theory, and ongoing case files.

They spoke of the 1947 Roswell crash. The sketches. The beings with immense black eyes and elongated limbs.

They spoke of the Arizona forester, who vanished for five days, reappearing pale and speechless, remembering only the sensation of being watched.

They spoke of Rendlesham Forest — "Britain's Roswell" — where soldiers saw glowing objects dart through the trees.

Then the Phoenix Lights of 1997 — V-shaped illuminations crossing the sky in eerie silence.

Then the *Belgian Wave* — 1989–1990 — triangular crafts, radar-confirmed, silent and unstoppable, witnessed by thousands.

And at last, the *Tic-Tac* UFO. 2004. Off the California coast. No engine. No wings. No sound. Captured by the U.S. Navy. Confirmed by the Pentagon.

"Who," asked Luca Romano softly, "is watching us?"

Then Dr. Nakamura spoke of the *Ancient Astronauts*. The pyramids. Stonehenge. The Nazca Lines — visible only from the air. Messages written in sand and stone. Markings for watchers above.

He spoke of Atlantis — not as a myth, but as a memory. Not drowned by disaster but silenced by design.

Later, Sophie Duval took the floor to speak of the dream of interstellar travel. The *Perpetual Motion Engine*. Suspended animation. Time dilation. A Moon base. Mars. Europa. Beyond.

Romano followed with the mystery of Crop Circles. Not hoaxes — not all. Some bore electromagnetic residue. Some formed astronomical maps.

"A warning?" he asked. "Or a welcome?"

The candlelight dimmed. The room softened. Their minds wandered — through time, through stars, through myth and science.

And as the final toast was raised, they spoke together, not as strangers, but as seekers:

"To the extraterrestrial meridian.
To the stars.
And to Mars."

The moon hung low, luminous. It watched, listening.

Then — silence. A flicker. A hum beneath the stone floor. The main screen blinked on.

Not an image.
Not a sound.
A pattern.

Pulsing.

Measuring.

Waiting.

And in that moment, every head turned skyward — not in wonder.

In recognition.

Something — or someone — had just replied.

STORY 5: THE SWISS MASQUERADE

A Tale of Love, Murder, and Song

The head of a jewelry store chain in Switzerland, Mr. Flauberg, sat in his office examining precious gemstones. He was seventy-two years old. Befitting his status, he was lean—almost wiry—with a neatly cropped haircut of silver-gray hair, gleaming with a striking metallic sheen. When he walked with his brisk, athletic stride, women often turned to glance at him, drawn to the confident gait of a man who had mastered success.

Mr. Flauberg had been married for only ten years to the stunning Astrid, a native of Salzburg, Austria. She was fifty but could easily pass for thirty. Astrid had been an opera singer, and when she married Mr. Flauberg, she left her beloved Salzburg—the city where she had grown up—and moved to the rather dull, staid city of Bern in Switzerland.

The two led largely independent lives, rarely infringing on each other's interests. For the most part, their communication consisted of phone calls or brief text messages. Astrid, however, had a charming lover, Serge, barely past thirty, who was perpetually in need of money. Astrid, tirelessly devoted to him, would gift him watches from renowned Swiss brands coveted by collectors or, more often, simply give him cash, as she seldom had time to buy her favorite companion the extravagant presents, he deserved.

On this rather overcast day at the end of August, Astrid decided it was time to visit her plastic surgeon—not to fix anything, but to fine-tune her already flawless appearance. Astrid had no flaws to speak of, and she was meticulous in ensuring that the passage of time left no mark upon her.

When she and Mr. Flauberg attended the premiere of an opera at La Scala in Italy, heads invariably turned. Together, they looked better than American Hollywood stars.

It must be said that neither of their lives was lacking in any way. They never cared for anyone but themselves, which is precisely why they had never taken the time to have children. Perhaps Mr. Flauberg had fathered illegitimate children across the globe, but if so, he had never given them a moment's thought. He was content with his life as it was. His one great love was for precious stones—rubies, sapphires, emeralds, and diamonds—and they loved him back in kind. Astrid, on the other hand, had no interest in heirs, unwilling to risk her figure for the sake of motherhood.

Both had large families. Astrid hailed from a prosperous Austrian family in the picturesque city of Salzburg. Mr. Flauberg was born in neutral Switzerland and now stood at the helm of a jewelry store empire.

And so, Astrid set off to see her surgeon—renowned across Europe. "With any luck, she'll be occupied for three days," Serge thought to himself, a sly smile crossing his face. At the same time, he remembered his promise to meet his young Latvian mistress, Annette, who was all of nineteen.

Annette was a pretty girl, though entirely unsettled in life. The first time Serge met her was in a café. He'd brought her back to his apartment on a night when heavy rain lashed the streets, and she had been shivering from the cold. For reasons he couldn't quite explain, Serge had felt sorry for Annette and offered her a separate room in his luxurious apartment. He handed her a plush, warm bathrobe and invited her to wash up.

Annette stepped into the expansive bathroom, her eyes widening at the sight of the rows of bottles—lotions for the body and face, shampoos, and stacks of large, fluffy towels. She gasped audibly, then began brushing her long, slightly wavy hair. She washed her hands, slipped her head under the stream of cold water for a moment, and then took a sip of sparkling mineral water before finally deciding to take a shower.

Annette had come to Europe from Latvia and had somehow cunningly managed to find her footing in Switzerland. Yet, she was still without proper documents or a permanent place to stay, constantly moving from one location to another. Her journey had begun in France, where she had arrived in hopes of making it as a model. But her appearance at the time—scruffy and disheveled—had left the agency unimpressed, and she was dismissed as having no potential.

Annette had a soft, curvaceous figure that was well-proportioned in all the right places. Her face was speckled with vibrant ginger freckles, giving her a youthful charm, though her hair, unkempt and sticking out in various directions, only added to her unpolished appearance. She often dreamed of visiting a hair salon for a proper cut, but she lacked the money to do so.

She suffered from loneliness, with no friends to confide in about her struggles. Despite her isolation, Annette's most remarkable quality was her unwavering smile. At just nineteen years old, she still had time on her side. She was healthy, full-figured without being overweight—what one might even call pleasantly plump. Serge often wondered how she could smile so brightly when she had no one and nothing to her name. It seemed to defy all logic, but Annette smiled nonetheless, as though challenging the world to dull her spirit.

Serge had brought her back to his apartment, then left her alone in one wing of the sprawling residence. Before he left, he set down a large sandwich with cheese and a bottle of sparkling mineral water, ensuring she wouldn't go hungry.

But today, Serge was troubled by Annette's recent comments about wanting children. He had even noticed that she seemed to have gained a little weight. For a brief moment, he entertained the thought of marrying her—having healthy children together, building a life. But the reality of his situation loomed large. He knew all too well what he stood to lose. If Astrid discovered that he had married someone else and was expecting a child… the consequences would be catastrophic. Serge could already see it: the financial support he relied on would disappear overnight.

And then another thought struck him—a dark, unsettling one. It felt as though all of Europe had come to a standstill. Life had grown difficult, even dangerous in some ways. That sense of unease made it even harder for him to make such a monumental decision as starting a family.

Meanwhile, let us return to Monsieur Flauberg. That same day, he traveled to Milan. At the appointed hour, he met with his intermediary, a representative from a firm that sourced and traded precious gemstones from around the globe. Monsieur Flauberg took the elevator up to the fourth floor and entered the office of Mr. Mannenheim. The elevator doors opened directly into the office, where they sat down at a polished mahogany table.

As usual, they began their meeting with polite greetings, discussing the state of the world. Their conversation soon veered toward a familiar refrain: how fortunate they were to have already lived through most of their lives. They mused over the growing unrest in Europe, the waves of people migrating to Europe and America in search of a better life, and the chaos such movements would inevitably bring.

Monsieur Flauberg left Mr. Mannenheim's office quite late, around nine o'clock in the evening. He thought it might be a good idea to stop by a restaurant for a light meal. Sliding into the driver's seat of his sleek Lamborghini, he navigated the city streets until he reached an upscale establishment.

That evening, the restaurant was nearly empty. A young waitress approached him, dressed neatly in a crisp white blouse and a flared skirt that swirled lightly with her movements. She smiled warmly at Monsieur Flauberg and suggested the chef's special—a hot dish featuring scallops accompanied by a fresh green salad.

Monsieur Flauberg returned her smile, the ruby on his elegant ring catching the light and glinting brilliantly. The waitress, her smile unwavering, entered his order into her handheld device and hurried off to the kitchen.

Monsieur Flauberg was utterly captivated by the young waitress, and for a fleeting moment, he regretted not having met her earlier in life.

"She resembles the Madonna sculpture in our cathedral," he mused to himself. Against all reason, he felt a stirring within him—a desire to be near her. He was acutely aware that the vigor of his youth had long since abandoned him, yet he couldn't help but picture this young woman cradling a small child in her arms.

"Ah, of course," he thought with a faint smile. "That's the Raphael painting that adorns my study wall. It's as though she's stepped out of the canvas." Inspiration struck him suddenly. "I know what to do," he decided. "I'll give her my business card. That way, we'll have a reason to meet again."

Meanwhile, Astrid was in unusually high spirits. Despite the overcast day and the drizzle that had come and gone, she found herself strolling along the central boulevard of Lyon, France. It was a city she frequented often, and today, she felt an irresistible urge to visit her favorite café for a cup of rich black coffee accompanied by a slice of the world-famous Sacher torte.

The café was quiet, with only a few patrons scattered among its cozy tables. Soft music played in the background, and Astrid smiled as she recognized the familiar voice of her favorite tenor. He was an exceptional performer, known for his playful rapport with audiences. Occasionally, he would whistle between verses or flash a mischievous smile as he glided effortlessly across the stage.

"I simply must attend one of his concerts," Astrid thought, her excitement building at the prospect of seeing him perform live.

She sipped her coffee, savoring the deep, bitter richness, and then took her first bite of the famed Sacher torte. The velvety cream and glossy chocolate glaze melted on her tongue, filling her with a sense of pure indulgence. She closed her eyes in delight, let out a satisfied sigh, and glanced out the window. The rain had stopped, and the cobblestone streets of Lyon glistened under a tentative patch of sunlight.

Feeling inspired, Astrid decided to take a leisurely walk through the familiar streets. Perhaps she would step into one of the charming boutiques, find herself a new dress or a chic skirt—whatever caught her fancy.

As she wandered, her attention was drawn to a large shop window displaying an eclectic array of curiosities. Beyond the glass, she noticed a middle-aged woman with long, dark hair seated at a small table. The woman wore a colorful, flowing dress and seemed entirely at ease, sipping tea from a porcelain cup. There was something magnetic about her presence, a quiet confidence that made Astrid pause for a moment longer than she intended.

In the window hung a sign that read:

"Do not pass by. Here, you can learn your destiny and change it in the direction you desire. I am a fifth-generation seer. I will help you correct your life, reveal the truth, and name your friends and enemies. My name is Sophia. I speak all languages, understand everyone, and will show you the path to a better life."

Without hesitation, Astrid opened the door and stepped into a spacious room filled with fresh flowers and the fragrant aroma of Indian incense. The hostess, serious and poised, glanced at Astrid and greeted her in perfect German:

"*Guten Tag.* Please, take a seat."

The seer, Sophia, spoke without the faintest trace of an accent. Moments later, she seamlessly transitioned into French, leaving Astrid astonished.

"Impressive," Astrid thought, though she chose to respond in her native German.

Sophia asked no questions. Instead, she began speaking as though she already knew everything about her visitor.

"Soon, you will return to your hometown of Salzburg," Sophia said confidently. "You are a talented and well-established woman. You will never have children, but you will sing alongside a famous tenor very soon. It will be a serious romance. You are the same age. You are fifty, yet you could easily pass for thirty. You look wonderful. Use your talent, and you will captivate all of Europe. You will sing great arias, and they will bring you great success."

Astrid listened; her breath caught in her throat.

"But what about my husband, Günther Flauberg?" she suddenly asked.

"Do not worry about your husband," Sophia replied unexpectedly. "He has his own destiny."

Without pressing further, Astrid placed a stack of Swiss francs on the table. Sophia accepted the bills, counted them carefully, and slipped them into the pocket of her wide skirt. Closing her eyes, she added in parting:

"Take care of yourself. You will face difficulties and changes. Come back to me if you need help; I will do my best to assist you."

Meanwhile, Monsieur Flauberg, as usual, was seated in his office, admiring his latest acquisitions: colored corundum, emeralds, sapphires, rubies, and, of course, diamonds—some of which were colored as well. One sapphire, with a vivid cornflower-blue hue, seemed to illuminate the room with an almost ethereal, heavenly glow.

He glanced out the window. The rain had stopped, and flashes of sunlight played on the surfaces of the street, casting shifting, colorful reflections that appeared here and there before fading into darkness once more. Monsieur Flauberg thought to himself that the weather was fickle, and rain could be expected again. He enjoyed overcast days immensely—they lent themselves to quiet and coolness, making his work easier and more contemplative.

Among the gemstones, Monsieur Flauberg's eyes fell upon a ruby discovered in Tanzania. The gem, of extraordinary beauty, resembled a drop of blood against the pristine white background of the jewelry box where it was stored.

"This ruby must be acquired by the Vatican," he thought. Such a powerful stone deserved a worthy purpose—it would adorn the rings of Vatican priests, symbolizing authority and sanctity.

Monsieur Flauberg knew the value of rubies and wore one himself, set in an elegant ring. Rubies were known to signify power, might, and inner fire. Ancient texts preserved in the Vatican library spoke of the ruby's virtues: it granted its wearer the strength of a lion, the fearlessness of an eagle, and the wisdom of a serpent. It was said to enhance passion and the seductive allure of love.

For a moment, Monsieur Flauberg sat at his desk, contemplating the future. Then, a decision crystallized in his mind—he would write to Astrid, who was due to return home soon.

She needed to know the truth: that he had fallen in love, as though he were a young man again, and now wished to marry the young woman who had captured his heart. "Why not?" he thought. "I am healthy, wealthy, and the times demand that we seize life rather than stand still."

Rising from his chair, he retrieved a crisp sheet of paper and began to pen the letter.

"Dear Astrid," he wrote, pausing with a sigh. "What shall I write next? I must ask for a divorce. I believe this is best for everyone.

How is Serge doing? We live under the same roof, attend events together, yet we share nothing in common. I finally want a family and a child—a little angel to guide and nurture toward a worthy and happy life.

I ask you to take your jewelry and return to your hometown of Salzburg. I am leaving you the chalet in the Alps, where you can ski to your heart's content—you always loved the mountains. My lawyer will deliver the official documents; all you need to do is sign them, and you will be entirely free. You have your magnificent collection of jewels and your Alpine retreat. Youth and beauty are still on your side. As for Serge, I suggest you leave him behind and return to your career as an opera singer in your beloved Salzburg. Farewell, my dear. We made a big mistake and lost ten years of our lives."

Monsieur Flauberg—Günther—signed the letter with his distinctive, sweeping handwriting. He carefully folded it, placed it in an envelope, and sealed it with a special wax seal.

Astrid arrived in Bern and went straight to Serge's apartment without calling ahead. Strangely enough, he wasn't busy. His flat, as always, was a chaotic mess. When Serge opened the door, expecting a business associate he had been working with on a small perfume and skincare line for the renowned French brand *Guerlain*, he was surprised to see Astrid. She stood there, fresh, radiant, and exuding happiness.

Serge greeted her warmly, and the two laughed as if sharing a private joke. He lifted her effortlessly into his arms, carrying her through the cluttered, narrow hallway before gently laying her down on his wide bed. They both burst into laughter, their joy infectious and unrestrained.

Astrid woke early the next morning after a sleepless, passionate night. While Serge slept deeply, she slipped into the bathroom, splashed cold water on her face, and wandered back out, not bothering to check her reflection. She hastily pinned her tousled hair with a large plastic clip she had picked up in a French shop on her way there. Her mind was a fog of emotions, as if she were under the influence of some psychedelic trance.

The streets outside were mostly empty as she stepped into the pale morning light, donning oversized black sunglasses to hide her face. Thank goodness she managed to walk steadily in her high heels despite her mental haze. Eventually, she hailed a taxi, which carried her back to the mansion she shared with Monsieur Flauberg. The entire journey was silent; Astrid couldn't even recall paying the driver.

Arriving at the grand house, she opened the heavy front door and slipped inside, heading to her side of the residence. She had no desire to see Monsieur Flauberg and doubted she could discuss anything coherent with him at that moment. Her heart still pounded under the anesthetic haze of passion.

Once in her room, Astrid noticed a peculiar envelope lying on her desk. Picking it up, she immediately recognized the handwriting—it was Monsieur Flauberg's. Her heart sank. "What does this mean?" she wondered, her hands trembling as she opened the envelope and began to read the letter.

Her pulse quickened as she clutched her head, ripping off her sunglasses in shock. Suddenly, her daze cleared. With Monsieur Flauberg, there was no room for jokes. She had brazenly carried on her affair with Serge, ignoring the swirling rumors and gossip that always surrounded her.

She stepped into the bathroom, washed her face, and drank a glass of water before returning to her desk. She unlocked the heavy safe hidden in the corner of the room by inputting the secret code, and its thick door creaked open. From inside, Astrid retrieved three large jewelry boxes and tossed them into a spacious travel bag. Without sparing a thought for her wardrobe or evening gowns, she slipped on a pair of sneakers, called a car service, and booked a ticket from Geneva to Salzburg. She wanted to leave the cold mansion immediately—every second spent there felt unbearable.

"I'll sing again in Salzburg," she thought as she closed the heavy front door behind her. A car waited at the entrance, and the driver kindly helped her into the vehicle. "To the airport," she instructed, and the driver wordlessly took her to the local terminal.

On the way, Astrid asked the driver to stop at a nearby bank. She spent about thirty minutes there, securing the three jewelry boxes in a safety deposit box. "This is for the best," she thought. Monsieur Flauberg would sort out his feelings soon enough.

"He's lost his mind, that's all. It happens to everyone at some point. The key is not to argue and simply do as your lawful husband says," Astrid mused, feeling strangely liberated and unburdened as the taxi continued toward the airport.

Her flight was a series of connections—no direct route was available, much to her annoyance. During the journey, the man seated beside her, a pleasant-looking middle-aged gentleman dressed casually in jeans, a leather jacket, and a white T-shirt, struck up a conversation with her.

At first, Astrid brushed the man off as if he were an annoying fly. However, as the fog in her mind began to lift, she engaged in conversation. The man introduced himself as Thomas, an American military officer working at the Marshall European Center for Security Studies in Garmisch-Partenkirchen, Bavaria, and the Edelweiss Lodge and Resort in the Alps.

Astrid soon found herself chatting animatedly. By the time they landed in Geneva, she was in high spirits. She bid Thomas a warm farewell, taking his business card before boarding her connecting flight to Salzburg.

"Well, this isn't so bad," she thought with a relieved sigh. "I should've expected this," she added to herself, only to promptly forget about Thomas. "I must focus on myself above all else," she said aloud, reinforcing her resolve.

Astrid arrived home late that evening, to her apartment on the fifth floor of a building nestled in a park-like area. The balcony, as always, was decorated with colorful flowers. She took the elevator up, opened the door, and stepped into the apartment she hadn't visited in ages.

Flicking on the lights, she froze for a moment, closing her eyes. Familiar scents filled the air, and even the passage of time hadn't dulled the fragrance of the antique paintings adorning the walls. There were works by Pablo Picasso, Marc Chagall, Joan Miró, and Salvador Dalí, as well as numerous German and French masterpieces stored away in the apartment's archives.

Astrid removed her clothes, slipped into a velvet, deep-maroon robe, and made her way to the kitchen. She found some ground coffee and a copper cezve, brewing herself a coffee with a thick, fragrant foam. She took the cup to the flower-bordered balcony and gazed at the breathtaking landscape that had been etched into her memory since childhood.

After finishing her coffee, she headed to the bathroom, stepping into a long, hot shower. She stood there for what felt like forever, as if washing away the haze and chaos of the day. Wrapping herself in a plush terry robe, she went into the living room, collapsed onto her favorite sofa, and fell into a deep sleep.

It was late at night when the darkness stirred her awake. Groggily, she made her way to the bedroom and slept soundly until morning.

The next day, Astrid's peace was abruptly shattered by two unsettling letters. The first was from Monsieur Flauberg's attorney. The second was an official summons from the police.

With a growing sense of dread, she opened the letter from the police. It informed her that Serge Marois, her French lover, had died suddenly during the night. A toxicology report revealed lethal poison in his bloodstream, and his apartment had been robbed of its most valuable possessions: luxury watches from Piaget, Vacheron Constantin, Jaeger-LeCoultre, Hermès, Franck Muller, Cartier, Chopard, and Bulgari.

Astrid's face turned pale as she clutched her head in shock. She realized she had no solid alibi. If she didn't act quickly, she could find herself implicated.

"I'll have to return to Bern and face the police," she thought, her mind racing. "But who could've done this? Who would rob Serge?"

Her thoughts spiraled as the enormity of the situation sank in. The idea of going back to Bern filled her with dread. "I want to call it a prudish backwater where even sitting or standing wrong seems forbidden," she muttered under her breath.

"I need a lawyer, of course, but there's more," she realized. "Monsieur Flauberg and his demands will complicate things."

Astrid decided on two immediate courses of action: first, she would call Thomas, the American military officer she had met on the plane. He might be able to offer advice or assistance through his network. Second, she would visit Sophia, the clairvoyant she had met in Lyon, whose insights might shed light on her precarious situation.

Finally, she would notify the Bern police, explaining that she was currently far from the city and could only arrive in two days.

Astrid dressed simply, choosing practicality over elegance, though her outfit retained an air of understated luxury. She wore her diamond wedding ring on one hand, paired with antique diamond earrings and her favorite golden Baume & Mercier watch with a mother-of-pearl dial. Slipping into leather flats, she grabbed her small travel backpack and ordered a taxi to the airport. Her destination: Lyon, where she hoped Sophia, the clairvoyant, could help her untangle the threads of her life.

She moved quickly, almost as if flying toward Sophia, and when she saw the silhouette of the clairvoyant through the shop window, she felt an inexplicable wave of relief. Without bothering to knock, Astrid entered the cozy parlor on the first floor.

Sophia, calm and composed, turned her gaze to Astrid and said, "I was expecting you. You've tied a Gordian knot in your life, and your husband has only tightened it. But don't worry—he won't hinder you in the end. Sit down, rest. I'll read the signs, and all will become clear."

Sophia closed her eyes, her expression serene, before slipping into what appeared to be a trance. A moment later, soft snores filled the room.

Astrid, sitting stiffly in her chair, wasn't sure whether to feel amused or uneasy. Was Sophia asleep or journeying to another realm? Before Astrid could decide, Sophia's eyes snapped open.

"Listen to me," Sophia began, her tone sharp and precise. "Your husband has no part in Serge's death. He doesn't need to kill anyone, least of all your former lover. He'll get his divorce from you without trouble. But mark my words—his path won't be smooth. There's a nineteen-year-old girl from Latvia involved, and she has family—

relatives who will use this situation to their advantage. She plans to have his child and bring her mother and sister to Switzerland. Your husband is not prepared for the chaos this will bring. He's used to dealing with wealthy, agreeable people—not with families from the Baltic states unfamiliar with the orderliness of neutral Switzerland."

Sophia paused, her gaze unwavering. "But enough about him. Serge's death was not random. He was poisoned with a potent toxin by a business partner—one who envied him, robbed him, and took an enormous batch of luxury watches. That man is now selling the stolen timepieces to fences across France. Many of these criminals store their goods in underground hideouts, as they've done for centuries. Serge was far too trusting, always boasting about his collection of watches, some of which are worth millions. That partner saw an opportunity and took it."

Reaching behind her, Sophia picked up a small vial and handed it to Astrid. "Drink this," she said softly. "It will calm your mind. You'll be ready to face the police in Bern. By the time you arrive, they'll already be following the trail of Serge's business partner. Serge was charming, lighthearted, and friendly traits that made him both loved and envied. His openness led him to tragedy. Now, we must pray for the repose of his soul."

A tear slipped down Astrid's cheek as she crossed herself. She reached into her purse and pulled out a photograph of Serge, taken on the beach. His sun-kissed skin, bright blonde hair, and shining blue eyes seemed to leap out of the image, bringing the memories back in an overwhelming rush. Unable to contain her grief, she began to sob.

Sophia watched her for a moment before speaking gently. "There is someone else you should meet—Thomas, the American you encountered on your flight. He will be a good friend to you, and perhaps something more in time. Seek him out. But for now, let this chapter close. Come back to me in a few days. I trust you'll have good news."

Astrid composed herself, wiping her tears, and reached for her wallet. She placed a generous sum of money on Sophia's table. Then, after a brief hesitation, she opened her travel bag and removed a small velvet box.

"This is for you," Astrid said, her voice filled with gratitude. "It's a precious brooch, a family heirloom. My great-grandfather brought it to Salzburg from the Ural mines in Russia. It's very valuable."

Sophia took the brooch reverently, pinning it to her large floral shawl. The centerpiece was a ruby bud surrounded by intricate green petals, forming a delicate rose design.

"Thank you," Sophia whispered. "May my prayers guide you and bring you peace."

Astrid stepped out into the streets of Lyon, her mind heavy but her steps purposeful. Without hesitation, she flagged down a taxi and said, "To the airport." Soon, she found herself aboard a half-empty plane bound for Bern, Switzerland.

By the time she landed, the summons from the police was waiting for her. Astrid knew the conversation ahead would not be easy. Feeling the weight of the situation, she called her lawyer, asking for an urgent meeting. The appointment was set for the next day at his office in the old quarter of the city.

Sitting alone in her hotel room that evening, Astrid reflected on how rapidly her life had unraveled. Just days ago, she had been enjoying the comfort of her home and the thrill of small indulgences. Now, she found herself entangled in a whirlwind of accusations, secrets, and uncertainty. Though fear lingered, a stubborn resolve began to take root. She would face whatever awaited her and forge a new path, no matter how arduous.

The next morning, Astrid arrived punctually for her meeting. Her lawyer, a reserved but perceptive man, greeted her with professional courtesy. They went over every detail of her case, scrutinizing the circumstances surrounding Serge's death and the theft of the luxury watches. Together, they concluded that the best strategy was to collaborate with the police and provide any information that could aid their investigation. Time was critical, and Astrid understood the urgency. Every moment counted.

As she left the meeting, she felt a faint glimmer of relief. The clarity of a plan, however fragile, gave her a sense of direction. Returning to her hotel, she sat at the small desk in her room and wrote a letter to Mr. Flauberg. The message was brief but carried a resolute finality:

"Günther,
I received your letter. I agree to the divorce. Thank you for everything you've done for me. I am returning to Salzburg, Astrid."

Folding the letter carefully, she sealed it and arranged for it to be sent on the earliest morning flight. With the letter dispatched, all that remained was to wait for the next turn of events. She knew that nothing about her life would ever be the same, but for the first time in years, she felt ready to face the unknown.

To clear her head, Astrid stepped out of the hotel and wandered into a nearby café. The atmosphere was cozy, with soft music playing in the background and the aroma of freshly brewed coffee wafting through the air. She ordered a cup of coffee and chose a seat by the window, where she could watch the bustling streets of Bern.

As she sipped the rich, aromatic brew, her thoughts drifted to Salzburg. It was her hometown, a place of childhood memories and timeless charm. She hoped it would become a sanctuary, a place where she could rebuild her life and find the peace she so desperately needed.

Despite the uncertainty ahead, a quiet determination filled her. Life in Salzburg would not be easy, but Astrid felt the stirrings of a new beginning. She was ready to face whatever challenges lay ahead, her resolve as strong as the coffee in her cup.

Sitting in the café, Astrid's thoughts wandered back to Sophia's words: *"Your husband is not to blame. He had no reason to kill anyone, let alone your former lover, Serge."* The memory brought her a sense of clarity. The divorce from Günther was indeed the right decision. Astrid resolved that once she returned to Salzburg, she would dedicate herself fully to her career and perhaps find a way to rebuild her personal life.

Her reflections were abruptly interrupted by the soft chime of her phone. It was a call from the Bern police. The officer's voice on the line was measured but insistent, informing her that new evidence had surfaced in Serge's case and requesting her immediate presence for further questioning. Astrid felt her heart race, the sense of unease she had been holding at bay now surging to the forefront. She thanked the officer and ended the call, her hand trembling slightly as she set the phone down.

Returning to Bern meant another confrontation with the mounting troubles she was desperate to escape. Yet she knew she couldn't turn away. Gathering her resolve, Astrid paid for her coffee, hurried back to the hotel, packed her belongings, and set off for the police station.

Astrid stepped out onto the street, moving swiftly, her mind set. She flagged down a taxi, barely sparing a glance as she climbed into the back seat. "Bern, please, and quickly," she instructed the driver, her voice calm yet firm.

Settling into the plush leather seat, she closed her eyes, letting the hum of the engine and the rhythmic motion of the car lull her into a restless half-sleep. The highway stretched before them, wide and empty, allowing the taxi to speed along with unrelenting urgency. The countryside blurred by in streaks of green and gray as Astrid tried to steel herself for what lay ahead.

At the Bern police station, she was greeted by two detectives whose demeanor was as unyielding as their questions. The air of tension she had anticipated was replaced by an almost businesslike civility. They wasted no time delving into her past, probing her relationships with both Serge and Günther. Astrid answered truthfully, leaving out no detail—neither of her tumultuous affair with Serge nor of her intention to sever ties with Günther. The weight of her words hung heavily in the sterile interrogation room.

The lead investigator, Johann Weiss, a serious-looking man in his forties with a precise manner, ushered her into a private room.

"Good afternoon, Madame Flauberg," Weiss began, flipping open a thin folder bearing Astrid's name. His tone was even but authoritative. "Let's get straight to the point. Where were you on the night of August 13th into the morning of the 14th?"

Astrid froze, her composure faltering. Her face paled as she repeated the question aloud, buying herself time. "Where was I that night?" she echoed, her voice barely above a whisper. Finally, she drew a deep breath and met Weiss's gaze head-on. "I spent the night with Serge," she said firmly. "Afterward, I flew to Salzburg. On the 14th, I was already in Lyon, preparing for my flight back to my home city of Salzburg."

Weiss didn't blink. "And why did you suddenly decide to go to Salzburg, Madame? You live with your husband here in Bern, do you not?"

Astrid felt the ground shift beneath her. She gripped the armrests of the chair, her knuckles white. A wave of dizziness overtook her, and she found herself gasping for air. Seeing her distress, Weiss stood and retrieved a bottle of chilled mineral water from the mini fridge in the corner, along with a paper cup.

"Here," he said, placing the cup in front of her. Astrid sipped the water, her trembling hands betraying her growing anxiety. She sat in silence for a moment, then finally spoke.

"I went to Salzburg because I received a letter from my husband, Günther," she said quietly. "He demanded a divorce and instructed me to leave immediately for my hometown. He asked me to return to Salzburg, where I had lived and performed as an opera singer ten years ago."

After hours of questioning, the detectives shared their preliminary findings. Weiss nodded, his expression unreadable. "Very well," he said. "And on the same day, Serge, your… companion, was murdered. Poisoned, in fact."

Astrid flinched, her composure cracking at last. She ran a hand across her face, brushing away the tear that had formed in her eye. She had dreaded hearing those words spoken aloud, the finality of them cutting through her defenses.

"We've confirmed that Serge was poisoned," one of them stated, his voice steady but grave. "However, the identity of the perpetrator remains unclear. There are too many moving parts." They cautioned Astrid to remain in Bern until the investigation concluded and to refrain from disclosing any details to outside parties.

Weiss reached into the folder and produced several glossy photographs, spreading them out on the table before her. Each image depicted a collection of luxurious Swiss watches, their value apparent even in the grainy details of the prints.

"Do you recognize these watches, Madame?" he asked, his tone sharp.

"Yes, of course," Astrid replied, her voice steady but strained. "Serge loved watches. I gave him at least five as gifts. The rest... he purchased on his own, but I don't know where or how."

Weiss studied her closely before continuing. "And do you know a man by the name of Berger Urs? He is not a Swiss citizen but has been residing in Germany for some time. He was known to associate with Serge in recent months."

Astrid shook her head firmly. "No," she said. "I've never heard that name, nor have I met him at Serge's apartment or anywhere else."

Weiss leaned back in his chair, observing her carefully. Her responses, though unflinching, seemed rehearsed—yet not in a way that suggested guilt. Rather, she seemed deeply wounded, carrying a weight of grief that made her sincerity ring true.

"Madame Flauberg," he said at last, "Serge Murua was poisoned with a highly potent toxin. It was not an accident. This was premeditated murder."

Astrid's face drained of color once again. "I need more water," she whispered, her voice barely audible.

Weiss obliged, handing her another cup of water before stepping out of the room.

Outside, Weiss conferred with his junior colleague, Ludwig Stein. The two men exchanged clipped words; their discussion laced with urgency.

"We're closing in on Berger Urs," Weiss said. "He's been seen traveling between Bern and Frankfurt, selling off Serge Murua's stolen watch collection to fences in France and Germany. The man is brazen, ignoring every summons we've sent him."

Stein nodded, taking notes. "His pattern of movement matches the timeline," he agreed. "We've forwarded his dossier to the TIGRIS division for further action."

Inside the interrogation room, Astrid sat alone, staring at the stark white walls. Weiss returned moments later, his expression softer but his tone firm.

"Madame Flauberg, you may leave for now, but you are not permitted to leave Bern until the investigation is complete. We will need you for further questioning."

When she finally stepped out of the police station, the evening air felt heavy, pressing down on her shoulders. Relief washed over her momentarily—she had been cleared of immediate suspicion—but the uncertainty of what lay ahead loomed large. There was no denying that the path forward would be fraught with challenges.

At the Bern police station, Günther Flauberg arrived with his lawyer, Mikael Heineken, in tow. His usually composed demeanor was absent; he was visibly fuming. It wasn't just the betrayal—Astrid having an affair with Serge Murua under his roof, in his own mansion no less—that enraged him. Now, on top of this scandal, Günther found himself entangled in a murder investigation concerning Serge's poisoning.

"Why in heaven's name would I kill someone?" he ranted to his lawyer before the interrogation began. "If anything, they should be questioning that slimy swindler Berger Urs about the murder. Everyone should live and suffer—that would be far more fitting!"

Mikael Heineken, a seasoned lawyer from Frankfurt who had handled many of Günther's most delicate legal entanglements, nodded calmly. "Let me do the talking," he said as they entered the interview room.

The lead investigator, Johann Weiss, wasted no time. Günther's alibi was scrutinized in detail. Mikael produced a letter confirming Günther's whereabouts on the night of the murder. After a thorough review, the authorities released him, but Günther was required to sign an agreement not to leave Bern until the investigation concluded.

Astrid, meanwhile, was also instructed to remain in Bern until the killer was apprehended. The police now had strong evidence implicating Berger Urs in Serge's murder. The venom used—a highly potent and exotic snake toxin—was not something easily obtained. How Berger had managed to procure it, and through whom, remained a key question.

When she finally stepped out of the police station, the evening air felt heavy, pressing down on her shoulders. Relief washed over her momentarily—she had been cleared of immediate suspicion—but the uncertainty of what lay ahead loomed large. There was no denying that the path forward would be fraught with challenges.

While the investigation continued, Berger Urs, unaware of the police's progress, had set his sights on Astrid. From his hideout just outside Bern, he plotted his next move. He called her, disguising his voice.

"Madame Flauberg," he said smoothly, "I'd like to meet with you. I was well-acquainted with both Serge Murua and your husband, Günther. I have information you'll want to hear."

The meeting was arranged at a cozy café in Bern called the Black Rose. Astrid, her instincts sharp as ever, immediately alerted the police from an anonymous phone line.

"Someone claiming to know Serge is meeting me at the Black Rose café," she explained. The officer on the other end instructed her firmly: "Do not eat or drink anything he offers you. Do not touch any utensils or glasses he provides. We will be nearby in case of trouble."

Astrid agreed and thanked the officer. She prepared herself meticulously for the encounter. Staying at a central hotel in Bern, she ventured out to purchase a tailored dark suit and a pair of sleek heels. She even visited a salon to have her hair styled into an elegant chignon.

The Black Rose café was sparsely populated that evening, with a few patrons seated in private booths. Astrid arrived early and chose a table in the farthest corner, ensuring she had a clear view of the entrance. She ordered a sealed glass bottle of mineral water, as instructed, and waited.

Fifteen minutes later, the man arrived. He was tall and slim, dressed in a sharp suit with a white shirt unbuttoned at the collar. A leather briefcase swung from his hand as he entered. He appeared to be in his mid-fifties and wore glasses. His polished demeanor masked a cunning edge.

"Madame Flauberg," he said, approaching her with a charming smile. "A pleasure to meet you. My name is Johannes Järvinen." He extended his hand, and Astrid shook it cautiously.

The man wasted no time. He pulled a stack of photographs from his briefcase and spread them on the table. Each picture showcased expensive Swiss watches, their opulence unmistakable. Astrid's breath caught in her throat—she immediately recognized five pairs of watches she had gifted Serge.

"Well, Madame Flauberg," Järvinen said with a sly grin, "I'm offering you a chance to buy back these five pairs of watches for a mere half-million Swiss francs. It's a fair price, considering their worth. You can transfer the money to me this afternoon."

He leaned closer, his tone turning menacing. "If you refuse, I'll take this little story to Günther Flauberg. I'm sure he'd love to know that you spent your last night with Serge Murua, just hours before his untimely death."

Astrid's face flushed with anger, her hands balling into fists under the table. "Give me thirty minutes," she said coldly. "We'll meet back here, and I'll have an answer for you."

Järvinen nodded, dabbing sweat from his brow. "Good," he said, pulling out a printed slip from his briefcase. After adjusting his Cartier watch, Berger Urs handed over his banking instructions with a trembling hand.

"Here are my bank details. You'll wire the money to Berger Urs—this account is in Luxembourg. Don't delay, Madame."

Astrid snatched the paper, her lips curling into a bitter smile. Without another word, she left the café and hurried to a nearby bank. There, she met with a banker and transferred half a million Swiss francs into a newly opened account under her name. This precaution, she knew, would protect her assets from the sticky and manipulative hands of Berger Urs.

Astrid signed all the necessary documents at the bank. While speaking with the bank representative, she explained that in thirty minutes, she would be transferring, via e-banking, half a million Swiss francs to a third-party account in Luxembourg.

The banker, not batting an eye, handed Astrid a printed copy of the transfer instructions.

"There's no need to worry, Madame," he reassured her. "Everything will be done exactly as you wish."

Astrid left the bank and immediately dialed the International Investigations Division. Speaking directly with the lead investigator, she informed him that she was prepared to meet Berger Urs—posing as "Johannes Järvinen"—at the local café in fifteen minutes.

"Thank you for letting us know," the officer said. "*Auf Wiedersehen.* Don't worry, we'll be nearby."

Astrid crossed the square quickly and, exactly thirty minutes later, was seated at the same secluded spot in the back of the café, waiting. She sat motionless, her heart racing, until she saw Berger Urs approaching from a discreet table hidden behind a large tree.

She knew that this time Berger Urs—the man who had coldly murdered his longtime business partner—would arrive with her late boyfriend Serge's prized watch collection.

The man was visibly tense, dabbing sweat from his brow as he entered the café. He dropped heavily into the chair opposite Astrid; his head hunched into his shoulders. Without a word, he pulled out the watches and laid them on the table.

Astrid inhaled sharply. The collection was as breathtaking as it was heartbreaking. There they were—the exquisite watches she had lovingly gifted Serge, each one a vessel of memory.

First came the Vacheron Constantin Égérie Moon Phase Diamond-Pavé Watch, crafted from 18k white gold with a satin strap and three carats of diamonds, priced at 62,000 Swiss francs. Then, the stunning Roger Dubuis Excalibur Sottozero Skeleton Flying Tourbillon Watch, limited to just 88 pieces, worth a staggering 174,500 francs.

The watches kept coming, their opulence a painful reminder of her loss:

- Franck Muller's Vanguard Watch, 38,000 francs, with 620 brilliant-cut diamonds totaling 5.56 carats, set in 18k rose gold.

- Jaeger-LeCoultre's Master Ultra-Thin Tourbillon, 18k rose gold with a brown alligator strap, 68,000 francs.

- Cartier's Ballon Bleu de Cartier Watch, set with 126 brilliant-cut diamonds, in 18k pink gold, worth 58,500 francs.

- Chopard's Happy Diamonds Joaillerie Butterfly Watch, 18k white gold with a mother-of-pearl dial and 46 diamonds, priced at 31,800 francs.

Astrid stared at the watches, her heart heavy. She thought of Serge—his love for beautiful things and his carefree spirit. None of these treasures could ever fill the void he had left.

"Well," Berger said smoothly, "as you can see, I'm asking you for less than their worth. These watches are priceless to the right collector. I'll make it simple for you—transfer the money to my account, or I'll ensure that Günther Flauberg hears every detail about your last night with Serge Murua. The choice is yours."

Astrid's face flushed with anger, but she managed to maintain her composure.

Holding the bank slip with his account details, her lips curling into a bitter smile, Astrid swiftly transferred half a million Swiss francs to his Luxembourg account using her laptop.

Though it pained her to comply with Berger Urs's demands, she knew it was the only way to recover Serge's watches—and perhaps even bring his murderer to justice.

Minutes later, Berger Urs received confirmation of the transfer on his phone. He abruptly stood from his chair at the café and exited without so much as a word.

Berger Urs stepped into the alley, the cold air biting at his skin. The confirmation of the transfer had arrived—half a million francs, clean and untraceable. Yet, instead of relief, a familiar unease settled in his gut. He had played this game for years, always staying one step ahead, but something felt different this time. The walls were closing in, and he could almost hear the distant echo of footsteps trailing him. Clutching his coat tighter, he disappeared into the shadows, the weight of his choices pressing heavily upon him.

The three officers from the TIGRIS division, stationed in an unmarked car across the street, watched his silhouette dart through the alley and vanish into the night.

One officer muttered, "How does he keep slipping away like that? It's like he's a ghost."

"Where did he go?" the other officer added, scanning the area. "It's like he evaporated into thin air."

Back at the police station in Bern, investigators were piecing together Berger Urs's movements. They had learned that just days before Serge's murder, Urs had traveled to Hamburg—likely to procure the deadly toxin. The details of the transaction remained unclear, but the trail was growing ever more distinct.

The investigative team focused intently on unraveling the case, poring over the nature of the venom used in Serge's murder. All evidence pointed to Berger Urs. The toxin—a rare snake venom known as *curare*—had been acquired through underground channels, and tracing its source had become a critical step in the investigation.

Astrid walked down the hallway and entered the chief investigator's office. The officer behind the desk looked up, surprised but composed.

"Good afternoon," he said, gesturing for her to take a seat.

"My name is Astrid Flauberg," she began, her voice slightly unsteady. "I need to speak with you about the murder of my friend Serge Murua."

The investigator nodded. "Yes, Madame Flauberg. We understand you recently met with Berger Urs, who was operating under the alias 'Johannes Järvinen.'"

Wordlessly, Astrid reached into her bag and pulled out the watches. She arranged them on a black velvet display cloth the officer had laid out. The investigator couldn't help but admire the stunning collection, though his expression remained professional.

"These watches belonged to Serge," Astrid said, her voice trembling with fatigue. "I gave them to him as gifts. He treasured them. But today, I was forced to pay for them twice. I had to transfer half a million Swiss francs to Berger Urs to get them back."

The officer sighed, jotting down notes. "We know," he said gravely. "Now our task is to track Berger Urs and gather enough evidence to arrest him for Serge's murder and the theft of his collection."

"Madame Flauberg," he continued, "I need you to always keep your phone accessible. Should Berger Urs contact you again, inform us immediately. We'll provide you with a secondary phone for secure communication."

Astrid nodded, handing over a card with her hotel's address. "I'm staying at the Central Hotel," she said. "You'll know where to find me."

"Thank you for your cooperation," the investigator replied. "One more thing—Serge's body will be released for burial only after the investigation concludes. I'm sorry for the delay, but we need every detail to ensure justice is served."

Astrid left the station with a heavy heart, clutching Serge's watches tightly. She vowed to see this through to the end—for Serge's memory and for the truth.

She rose from her chair unsteadily. In the past few days, she had eaten almost nothing—only coffee and mineral water had passed her lips. "Thank you again. Auf Wiedersehen," she said softly, her voice tinged with exhaustion, before slowly leaving the investigator's office.

She wandered the streets for a while before finding herself in a familiar café where she and Serge had often shared coffee and homemade pastries. This time, she ordered a slice of berry crumble topped with a dusting of sugar. As she finally began to relax, her smartphone's melodic ringtone interrupted her thoughts.

Annoyed, Astrid picked up the phone and sighed, "Yes? Who is it?" She muttered to herself, irritated that she couldn't even enjoy a moment of peace. However, when she answered again, her voice had regained its composure: "I'm listening."

On the other end of the line was someone she recognized immediately: the lawyer who often handled Günther Flauberg's legal matters. His tone was overly familiar, almost playful.

"Dear Astrid," he began smoothly, "I understand you've found yourself in a rather troubling situation. Allow me to help you. I've been asked by Mr. Flauberg himself to step in and represent your interests in this matter. You see, Berger Urs is now the central figure in this case, and his sudden disappearance complicates everything. If he doesn't turn up for a meeting with you, things may drag on even longer."

The lawyer's voice lowered slightly, as though sharing a secret. "Everyone now knows that Berger Urs poisoned Serge Murua. Not only that, but he's been spotted traveling to France, attempting to sell off the stolen treasures from Bern."

Astrid remained silent, her grip tightening on the phone.

"So, here's what I suggest," the lawyer continued. "Mr. Flauberg will cover my fees, so there's no need for you to worry about the financial burden. Besides," he added with a chuckle, "I have a deep admiration for you, and I'll do everything in my power to resolve this matter swiftly. In fact, the Swiss legal system—famously neutral, as you know—is on your side. This case, Astrid, will ultimately concern everyone except you and Mr. Flauberg."

For the first time in days, Astrid felt a flicker of relief. The lawyer's confident words steadied her. She responded graciously, "Thank you very much. When should I come to your office to sign the necessary documents?"

"Please stop by tomorrow," the lawyer replied cheerfully. "I'll be in my office here in Bern. And don't worry about a thing—I mean it. This is an unfortunate mess, but I promise to sort it out entirely. Oh, and Astrid," he added in a lighter tone, "when you perform in Salzburg, do remember me. I adore the opera!"

Astrid couldn't help but smile faintly. "Thank you," she whispered, ready to end the call. The lawyer said his goodbyes, and she finally turned her attention back to the steaming slice of berry pie on her plate.

For the first time in days, Astrid allowed herself to savor the moment. She finished her pie slowly, enjoying every bite. The creamy scoop of melting vanilla ice cream beside it felt like a small luxury she hadn't allowed herself in what felt like ages. As she scraped up the last spoonful of ice cream, she leaned back in her chair, feeling momentarily at ease amidst the chaos of her life.

Sleep evaded Astrid that night. Instead, she walked to the coffee machine in her small hotel room and poured herself a cup into a disposable paper cup. The coffee lacked the richness she was used to —the smooth brew with a velvety foam that came from her favorite copper cezve. She abandoned the cup untouched and went to the bathroom, where she took a refreshing contrast shower. Feeling slightly more awake, she dressed quickly in jeans, a plain white T-shirt, and her trusty Adidas sneakers.

Moments later, a hotel attendant brought her the morning papers. As she unfolded the top newspaper, her eyes landed on the bold headline covering nearly the entire front page. It was about Berger Urs, the German living in Frankfurt. The German police had obtained a warrant to search his apartment and arrest him, but when they entered the premises, they discovered a mutilated corpse. The body had yet to be identified. The apartment itself was completely empty—not even furniture remained.

The report ended with an analysis from the TIGRIS international crime unit in Bern: the case had taken a shocking turn. Now, investigators not only needed to find Berger Urs's killer but also the missing stash of luxury Swiss watches—brands of unparalleled value and reputation.

Determined, Astrid called the police station and asked for the investigator in charge of the Berger Urs case.

"Yes, this is Investigator Weiss," came the measured reply.

"Good morning, this is Astrid Flauberg," she began, skipping pleasantries. Her voice was calm but urgent. "I've just read the latest news about Berger Urs in the papers. Is it true? Is the case officially stalled?"

The investigator cleared his throat before answering. "Mrs. Flauberg," he began cautiously, "while we cannot confirm all details yet, the case is indeed at a standstill. However, I can tell you this—you and your husband, Mr. Flauberg, are officially free to leave. There's just one condition."

Astrid held her breath as he continued.

"Since forensic analysis on the body discovered in Frankfurt has yet to be completed, we cannot completely rule out the possibility that this is a staged scene. As such, we advise you to remain vigilant. It's possible that new players may emerge—individuals you don't know—who might attempt to contact you and continue the extortion."

"For now, though, we have no further claims or demands on you. All we ask is that you answer any calls from unknown numbers and report them to the police immediately. The case is now focused on one objective: finding the stash of watches. We believe the collection may be hidden somewhere in France, and its value is estimated at approximately ten million francs—or perhaps even more.

"And one more thing, Mrs. Flauberg," the investigator added with a note of solemnity. "You are the rightful heir to this treasure, given the circumstances. Rest assured, we will support you in this matter. Please keep us informed of any developments."

"Thank you," Astrid whispered, her voice soft and measured. "I will be driving to Salzburg today, and I promise to stay in touch. You know my address. Please don't hesitate to send me any additional updates."

As she hung up the phone, Astrid sat in silence for a moment, absorbing everything. Finally, she spoke to herself, her tone laced with irony, "Well, it seems we've reached the beginning of the end."

As she walked through the dimly lit streets, Astrid resolved to face whatever came next with unrelenting determination. Each step brought her closer to a life she had yet to rebuild, even as the shadows of her past threatened to follow her.

Astrid returned to her hotel that night in Bern with an unusual sense of clarity. The police inquiry had been draining, yet Sofia's words echoed in her mind, urging her to seek the life awaiting her in Salzburg. That night, sleep eluded her. Instead, she sat by the window, watching the rain streak down the glass. She envisioned herself standing on a grand stage, bathed in light, her voice soaring into the heavens alongside the famous tenor Sofia had mentioned. It was a life that seemed distant, yet tantalizingly within reach.

By morning, Astrid had made her decision. The investigation into Serge's death was no longer her burden to carry. She would inform the authorities of her plan to leave Switzerland and return to Salzburg, where the foundation of her new life awaited.

With her heart lighter than it had been in months, Astrid boarded a train bound for Austria. The rhythmic hum of the wheels on the tracks lulled her into a state of calm, a rare peace that contrasted sharply with the turmoil of recent weeks. She thought of Günther's letter, the wealth of jewels she had locked away in the Geneva bank, and the memories she would leave behind in Bern. These remnants of her past no longer felt like burdens but steppingstones, leading her to something greater.

When the train pulled into Salzburg, Astrid felt a deep, nostalgic ache. The city welcomed her with its quaint cobbled streets, baroque architecture, and the distant sound of violins echoing from street performers. She took a cab to her apartment, which overlooked the verdant hills she had grown up admiring. As the sun set over the hills, painting the skyline in hues of amber and violet, she felt the weight of her past lift, replaced by the delicate anticipation of what lay ahead.

Weeks passed, and Astrid slowly settled into her new rhythm. She resumed voice training with an old mentor, a retired soprano who marveled at how Astrid's voice had matured. Word of her return spread, and before long, she was invited to an exclusive gala hosted by the Salzburg Opera Society.

That evening, wearing a simple yet elegant black gown, Astrid found herself introduced to none other than Leonardo Montavelli, the legendary Italian tenor. His presence was magnetic, commanding attention without effort, and his piercing green eyes held a warmth that immediately put her at ease.

"I've heard about your voice, Madame," he said with a slight bow. "It would be an honor to sing with you."

His voice was like music itself, each word measured yet melodic. Astrid felt a flutter of nervous excitement, but her smile remained composed.

The offer was serendipitous, and within weeks, Astrid had signed a contract to join him in a performance of *La Traviata* at the *Teatro alla Scala* in Milan—a venue she had long admired from afar.

The weeks leading up to the performance were grueling yet exhilarating. Astrid poured every ounce of her energy into rehearsals, her voice blossoming under the guidance of the opera's renowned conductor. Each day brought new challenges, but also a growing sense of fulfillment. It was as though every note she sang carried her closer to the life she had dared to dream of. Leonardo, ever the professional, became not only her duet partner but also a confidant. His humor and encouragement became a source of strength, their partnership deepening with every rehearsal. Their voices intertwined in harmony, mirroring the deep bond they had forged.

On the night of the performance, Astrid stood backstage in a flowing crimson gown. The hum of the audience beyond the curtain was a living, breathing thing, fueling her anticipation. She closed her eyes, breathing deeply, and let the memory of Sofia's words center her: *"The world is waiting for your voice."*

When the curtain rose, the crowd erupted—drawn by the legend of Leonardo. His presence was magnetic. Admiration rippled through the hall like wind through silk.

But as the opera unfolded, it was Astrid who held them spellbound.

Her voice rose—soft, then soaring. Haunting. Triumphant. Every note laid bare a soul both broken and brave.

In *"Parigi, o cara,"* their voices met like old lovers reunited. Each phrase a thread. Each harmony a confession. The audience leaned in; breath held. Spellbound.

Astrid glanced at Leonardo. His eyes shone with pride. And in that gaze, she saw herself—not the wife of a tycoon, not the woman bruised by scandal. An artist. A flame reborn.

Then came the final crescendo.

A silence fell.

Complete. Reverent.

Then, a roar.

Thunderous applause shook the walls. Flowers rained like blessings. Leonardo took her hand and lifted it high.

She had conquered.

Backstage, reporters surged forward. Cameras flashed. Voices clashed. But Astrid slipped away—graceful, silent.

She needed a moment.

Alone in her dressing room, she stood before the mirror. No longer the wife. No longer the scandal. She saw only the artist. Reborn. Her voice. Her fire.

She leaned in, forehead resting on the glass. Her pulse raced. The crowd was gone. The music, still echoing in her bones, throbbed like a second heartbeat.

She closed her eyes.

She saw it all—the chaos, the love, the lies. The detours. The grief.

And yet—

She breathed in peace. Deep. Certain.

The woman she had been—the ornament, the afterthought—was gone. In her place stood something new. Stronger. Sharper. Unshaken.

Note by note, she had rebuilt herself. Aria by aria, she had reclaimed her voice.

She thought of Vienna. Paris. New York. The grand halls. The golden lights. She could see it now—no longer as fantasy, but as promise.

This was not destiny.

This was choice.

With steady hands, she adjusted her crimson gown. Her gaze held firm.

"This is only the beginning," she whispered.

At the gala dinner, Leonardo raised his glass. "To Astrid," he said, eyes shining.

"A rare flame in a world dulled by repetition."

Astrid smiled. Lifted her glass. "To new beginnings," she said softly.

"And the courage to embrace them."

From that night onward, her name echoed through Europe's great halls. Her voice wove its way into legend.

Sofia's prophecy had not merely come true—it had been earned.

She had turned sorrow into song. Regret into renewal. Past into power.

And each time the curtain fell, and the applause rose like thunder, Astrid would remember:

"You will conquer all of Europe with your voice."

And indeed, she had.

STORY 6: THE GIRL FROM ESTONIA

Gerda awoke in high spirits. She skipped to the open window—sunlight streamed brightly, and birds twittered merrily in the trees. *Today, at last, I shall fulfill my dream*, she thought. *I will go to Stockholm and hear the music of the Eurovision concert.*

In the kitchen, she toasted a slice of bread, spread it with strawberry jam, and placed it neatly on a plate. Meanwhile, rich black coffee brewed in a copper cezve, and its marvelous aroma wafted through the apartment where Gerda lived alone. Her mother had long since departed for Germany with a new husband, leaving Gerda to fend for herself from a tender age.

She was attending foreign language courses and dreamed of becoming a translator. Yet in her heart of hearts, Gerda loved to sing and dance. Sometimes she fancied the notion of becoming a performer—like ABBA! *What a marvel it would be to meet the band, to become a part of such a famous group!*

She turned before the mirror and smiled at her reflection. *I must hurry if I am to catch the morning ferry.* She donned a long-knitted skirt, a multicolored sleeveless top, and a sun-faded blue denim jacket. Slipping on comfortable leather shoes, she slung a small backpack over her shoulder and dashed outside.

Gerda walked briskly down the street and boarded the bus. Precisely thirty minutes later, she arrived at the harbor. On that Saturday morning at nine o'clock, a large crowd had gathered, awaiting the ferry that would carry passengers from Estonia directly to Stockholm. Gerda stood in line and soon stepped aboard.

Up on the upper deck, one could bask in the sea breeze and the brilliant sunshine. After about an hour, the ferry docked at the port of a Swedish city also within the Schengen zone. Upon disembarking, Gerda presented her new Estonian passport to a young police officer in uniform, who smiled warmly at the lovely girl. Gerda returned the smile and stepped onto the quay.

After a brief stroll through the city, she found the ticket booth, marked in bold letters: *EUROVISION CONCERT TICKETS*. She bought an expensive ticket near the stage—her entire month's earnings. Gerda worked as a barmaid, and her wages barely covered her living expenses, but her heart yearned for something greater. She longed for fame, for recognition.

She had a beautiful voice, undeniable talent, and striking looks. Her caramel-colored hair fell in soft waves upon her shoulders. At times, she would brush mascara on her lashes, and then her eyes, set like twin oceans beneath the sky, shimmered in blue brilliance. Her face always glowed with joy. With a lithe figure and long graceful legs, Gerda possessed all she might need to win the public's adoration.

But today must be something special, she thought. *I am in Stockholm —the city of my dreams.*

After wandering a while longer, hunger began to stir. She stepped into a cozy bar-restaurant and seated herself at a table. Perusing the menu, Gerda ordered fried fish in batter and a glass of Pilsner beer from the Czech Republic. A handsome waiter brought the food on a large plate, and the television in the bar played the Eurovision concert live.

On screen, a group from Tallinn performed—a charming ensemble of sun-kissed, fair-haired boys and girls, singing Estonian folk songs with spirited dances. At the end of their number, the audience erupted in applause, and the host remarked, *"We are always in search of new talent."*

Just then, a young man and woman approached Gerda, greeted her cheerfully, and introduced themselves as Hans and Annette. They immediately invited her to toast a friendship with a *Brüderschaft*. The fair-haired waiter brought them glasses of wine, and together they cried, *"Skål! Long live Sweden!"*

Gerda only sipped, hardly drinking at all, but was nonetheless astonished by the ease with which these strangers had approached her. She told them she had just arrived that morning on the ferry from Estonia. Hans and Annette exchanged a meaningful glance, then invited Gerda to join them at their summer house to spend the rest of the day—and perhaps stay the night.

Without hesitation, Gerda agreed. She had, after all, considered spending the night at the train station in a chair. This invitation spared her that discomfort. *Just one day*, she thought, *and tomorrow, after the concert, I shall return home on the last ferry. What a stroke of good luck!*

As they made their way to the restaurant's parking lot, Hans and Annette beamed kindly at Gerda. *What pleasant people*, she mused, *so warm and welcoming... and perhaps even wealthy.* They were well-dressed, both wearing light-washed jeans, pristine white shirts, and spotless athletic shoes.

They approached a sleek, silver-blue Toyota. Though Gerda knew little about automobiles, even a brief glance inside told her the car was luxurious—its interior upholstered in fine leather. *Classy*, she thought, her eyes falling upon Hans's wristwatch. 'Audemars Piguet!' she gasped inwardly. *More expensive than a Rolex!* Then she noticed Annette's wrist adorned with a delicate Baume & Mercier watch, the face inlaid with diamonds.

They drove along a wide highway, flanked by tall, dark pines. Annette smiled at everyone, and she and Hans often conversed in their native tongue, only occasionally addressing Gerda. The road lulled her, and weariness crept in. *This is madness*, she thought. *To climb into a stranger's car in a foreign land, headed who-knows-where beyond Stockholm.* She regretted not bringing along her school friend—at least then she wouldn't have been alone.

Roughly an hour passed before the car turned into a wooded parkland and came to a stop before a grand manor. A stone house stood beyond a wrought-iron gate. Hans pressed a button, and the gates opened slowly with a metallic groan.

"We've arrived," they said in English—a language common for communication in Scandinavia, where many speak it fluently beyond their native tongues.

"What a beautiful house," Gerda remarked.

As they followed the path to the door, the sky darkened. A chilly rain fell, mingled with hail—tiny ice pellets struck her face and tangled in her hair. The forest around them grew dim and silent. The path, bordered by evergreens, led to a heavy front door which opened with effort, revealing a marble-floored hall flanked by silent statues. A chill lingered in the air, and Gerda shivered.

"May I freshen up somewhere?" she asked.

They offered her a glass of cognac. She took a sip—warmth spread through her chest, soothing her nerves. *All is well now. I have a roof over my head and won't have to sleep at the station,* she consoled herself. *Thank heavens Mama doesn't know where I am… she'd raise such a storm. She always says I'm too naïve.*

The corridor stretched before her, lined with many closed doors. The house was eerily quiet, save for faint music drifting from the drawing room—ABBA's nostalgic voices echoing like ghosts from the past. *Let them have their fun,* Gerda thought. *A sandwich would be nice, though. For now, a splash of water and a deep breath will do.*

She found the bathroom—a grand chamber with an additional door tucked in one corner. She approached the sink, washed her face, and dried it with a waffle-textured towel. Catching her reflection in the mirror, she noted a strange look in her eyes—was it fear?

Suddenly, she heard screams. Muffled at first, then louder—a woman's voice, desperate and pained. Her heart pounded. She turned toward the other door, opening it with care to avoid creaking. It led to a staircase.

Gerda ran down the steps and flung open another door—this one to the outside. Without looking back, she bolted through a ravine and into the dense forest beyond. Rain lashed her face; wind howled in the trees. She whispered prayers beneath her breath. *Let them not follow me. I must reach the highway… or a village… or a church. Churches are always safe. I must run. I must survive.*

She ran until her limbs failed her, stumbling and gasping. But no one pursued. At last, she saw the distant glow of highway lights.

I must hitch a ride… but only with a city bus, she vowed. *Never again with strangers.*

Cars passed without stopping. Then, like a miracle, a bus slowed and opened its doors.

"What's happened?" the driver asked, peering at her soaked and trembling form.

Gerda poured out her tale. The driver nodded solemnly.

"I'll take you to the police station."

He delivered her to a small stone building, where patrol cars stood outside and warm light spilled through the windows. She offered him her business card: Gerda Sinkevicius, student of foreign languages, Tallinn, Estonia.

He smiled, waved goodbye, and drove off.

Inside, it was warm and welcoming. A pot of dark coffee bubbled in the corner. It was 11:30 at night. Gerda crossed herself. *If I'd stayed even a moment longer in that house… something dreadful would've happened.*

A policeman approached. One look at Gerda and he knew—she had fled from something terrible. Her soaked knitted skirt clung to her legs, but she scarcely noticed.

She was alive.

And her mother would never know.

Gerda was led into a quiet room—a square table, two chairs. Behind one sat a man of middle age, dark-haired, with kind brown eyes. He smiled warmly.

"Please, take a seat," he said, his tone gentle.

He asked a few simple questions. Gerda explained that she was a language student from Tallinn and had come to Stockholm for the Eurovision concert. "It is the city of my dreams," she added shyly. The investigator nodded. "You were wise to run and come to the police. Now, please—help us identify those involved."

He placed several photographs on the table—images of the mansion Gerda had escaped from. "Do you recognize this house?"

Gerda's eyes widened. "Yes. Yes, that's the one! Hans and Annette brought me there."

The policeman nodded grimly. "Tonight, those same two came to us, frightened. They too had heard a woman's screams from the house's lower levels. Hans had gained entry through a local housekeeper, who informed him the owners were away on holiday and had lent the keys to friends."

The officer's expression darkened. "But a body has been found. A young woman—mutilated, brutally slain. We do not yet know who did this. But we must act swiftly."

He turned over more photographs: "These are of the estate, owned by a Swedish magnate, Mr. Sonnenberg. He lives in Stockholm during the winter but summers on an island far in the Atlantic. The house is overseen by a local caretaker, and the staff consists of three middle-aged women—Katarina, Emma, and Anna-Lena. Stern, solitary women. They tend the rooms and keep the grounds."

"Visitors come and go," he continued, "none related to the magnate. His many children and grandchildren live abroad—in Luxembourg, Monaco, and Italy. The house remains largely uninhabited."

Police had searched the mansion thoroughly—especially the basement, the attic, and its secret cellars. In one subterranean room, they discovered a stairwell descending to a hidden chamber lined with iron cages. Strange tools and grim instruments lay scattered about, the air thick with a ghastly odor—perhaps a gas. The chamber was sealed for a day before forensics would enter with masks and extract footprints for analysis.

"Now we must question the estate manager," the officer concluded. On Tuesday, the caretaker appeared for questioning—a man named Algis Donatas. He was heavyset, poorly dressed, unshaven, with inflamed red eyes. An unpleasant sight. He spoke poor Swedish, and the officers questioned his origins.

Under persistent inquiry, it emerged that he was a laborer from Lithuania, recently arrived. He had no knowledge of foreign languages, seemed likely an alcoholic—or perhaps simply dim-witted. His large, calloused hands looked more like claws than fingers. He twitched constantly, scratching his face and fidgeting with his clothes.

The investigator studied him carefully. Despite his ignorance and disorderly manner, he had access to the estate. When the questioning was complete, the officer handed him a document of restricted movement—he was not to leave Sweden—and demanded his signature.

Then the investigator left the room and entered a chamber full of computers. There, he entered Algis's details and photograph into the system and received this report:

"Resident of a Baltic state. Previously convicted multiple times in Lithuania. Served five years in prison for hooliganism. Released early, fled to Sweden, and became caretaker of the estate owned by Mr. Sonnenberg. Age: sixty-five."

The officer then requested images of all known victims, both in life and death. He examined them with care. Most had been young girls —thin, fair-haired, aged fourteen to twenty—each slain with extreme cruelty.

Next, he requested the names and photographs of all visitors to the estate. Among them appeared one name of particular interest: Dr. Lars Magnusson, a charming middle-aged emergency surgeon working in Stockholm and its surroundings.

The investigator sent him a letter, summoning him for questioning. Time passed. No reply.

The killings had ceased, but the officer's instinct would not rest. He sent another letter, more urgent. Still, the doctor did not respond.

Perhaps he is overwhelmed by his duties, the investigator mused. Or perhaps he has moved… and the address is no longer valid.

A day's rest was proposed—but only a day—for new witnesses had stepped forward.

On Monday, the police station was bustling again. Witnesses had come forward, claiming they had seen a truck parked near the road that led to the secluded estate. One night, in the hush of darkness, a man in a heavy coat and knitted cap had loaded a large sack into the back of the truck, then climbed into the cab and driven off toward the thick woods.

A gamekeeper, hidden among the bushes while patrolling the reserve, had witnessed the event. Silently, he crept closer and captured video footage—clear enough to reveal the man's face beneath the cap. The image was chilling: large, wild eyes, a thick reddish beard, and an expression more beast than man. The officers gasped. We must find this man, they said. They began scouring records of forest rangers, hospitals, and mental health facilities, seeking any clue.

The lead investigator proposed a bold plan.

"We must bait him," he said. "A woman from our force—someone brave—will pose as a naïve girl, lured into conversation. She'll be wired, tracked, and ready."

Preparations were made. By Thursday, on the eve of a traditional midsummer festival—known for revelry, disguise, and ancient rites—the plan was in place.

The bar was crowded. Laughter, singing, the scent of grilled sausages and beer mingled with cigarette smoke. Women wore bright clothing—short skirts, plunging necklines—and many flaunted tanned skin and platinum hair. A girl sat at the counter, humming a tune from ABBA as it played loudly on the screen above. That girl was Monika, a policewoman in disguise—jeans, a white blouse, red lipstick, and beneath her clothing, a hidden transmitter. A man approached.

His age was hard to tell. Bald, with dark, bulging eyes and an unnaturally thick red beard—clearly false. A costume. But this was a festival. Disguises were common, laughter encouraged. No one questioned him.

He took Monika's hand and led her outside, toward the riverbank. She followed, calm and silent.

"What's your name?" she asked.

"What does it matter?" he replied.

He tried to pull her toward the water, but she resisted. When he tugged her again, she discreetly pressed the button inside her bra. The transmitter activated.

He shoved her toward a truck, struck her on the back. Monika twisted, driving her elbow into his gut. He gasped—but grabbed her again and threw her into the truck.

Inside were sacks, bundles—and one sack whimpered.

Monika froze.

A girl.
Alive.

She began untying the rope. At that moment, the truck lurched forward.

The girl burst from the sack, weeping, crying out: "He's the killer!"

Monika whispered, "You're safe. I'm with the police."

The truck sped along a forest road. Monika signaled again. Headquarters tracked the coordinates on a great screen.

"The truck's heading to the magnate's estate!" the chief shouted. "Deploy now!"

Inside the cab, the man removed his fake beard. His face was darker, smoother. He tugged a black cap over his bald head. Monika braced herself. She whispered to the girl, "Run to the highway the moment he grabs me."

The truck stopped. He opened the rear and reached in.

He lunged at Monika.

She screamed—loud and sharp, the signal for the girl to flee. The girl darted into the woods, through a ravine, toward the lights of the road.

Inside the truck, Monika fought. Though trained, she was tiring. He overpowered her, nearly binding her hands.

If he gets me below ground, I'm lost, she thought.

Suddenly—sirens. Police cars, flashing lights, tires screeching.

With a burst of strength, Monika drove her knee into his groin. He crumpled. She struck him again—this time on the head.

He slumped to the floor.
She leapt from the truck, running toward her comrades.
"There!" she cried, pointing. "In the truck!"
Three officers raced to the rear. Monika stood motionless for a moment, trembling—until the rescued girl found her, threw her arms around her, and sobbed: "God bless you. You saved me."

The next day, the news broke across Sweden. Officer Monika had saved a girl from a murderer. The man was revealed to be an illegal immigrant from Tajikistan, a fugitive with no address, no job, and a history of robbery, torture, and the murdering of young girls.

Greta Sinkevicius had returned safely to Tallinn, to her little, cozy apartment. Summer lay upon the city, and Greta resolved she would no longer serve behind the bar—she would find real work. She sent an application to a newly formed international firm for Baltic-

Scandinavian cultural exchange, offering her skills in Estonian, Finnish, and English.

Within a week, she received a reply—an interview invitation in Stockholm.
She dressed in care: a dark blue suit, a white silk blouse, her hair drawn into a bun to appear more mature. She flew on the first flight to Sweden.

At the airport, a young man in a business suit awaited her, holding a placard:
INTERNATIONAL ORGANIZATION — GRETA SINKEVICIUS.
"I'm Jonas Berg," he said. "Welcome. I'll take you to your hotel and assist with the documents. Tomorrow is your interview."

He handed her a hotel key and an envelope. "Your advance payment," he smiled. "Stockholm is a beautiful city. Explore it, enjoy it. Tomorrow, your future begins."

Greta climbed to her room in a glass-walled elevator. The bed was soft, the pillows large, the blanket light and warm. It felt just like a fairy tale, she thought.

The next morning was cold and rainy. She shivered, drank water, and took a bracing shower. Dressed in her new suit, she met Jonas in the lobby.

Today would begin with her interview. Afterward, a corporate celebration was planned—the opening of the joint venture uniting Sweden, Latvia, Lithuania, and Estonia... and soon, perhaps, Germany.

The meeting room was modest. There, Mr. Sture Svendberg and Bengt Karlsson, directors of the firm, greeted her warmly.
"Please, tell us a little about yourself," they said.

Greta stood, nervous but proud. "I've always dreamed of coming to Stockholm," she began. "And I'm honored to offer my skills as a translator and representative of this new company."

She added in English, "People in the Baltics speak many tongues, including Russian, but documentation is always kept in our native Estonian, Latvian, and Lithuanian."

The directors smiled. "Congratulations, Miss Sinkevicius. You begin Monday."

They handed her a key to a company-provided apartment and wished her success.

As Greta stepped out into the Stockholm morning, briefcase in hand and resolve in her heart, she paused beneath a sky still heavy with rainclouds. But to her, it was radiant. She was no longer the girl who had run through a storm, barefoot and trembling. She was a woman who had faced darkness and chosen light. The city she once feared had become the place where her life would begin anew—not in song or fantasy, but in strength, in purpose, and in the quiet, unshakable dignity of survival.

STORY 7: NORDLYS—THE NORTHERN CODE

Elsa, a resident of Estonia, met a Norwegian captain in the spring of 1937, at the beginning of May. A long-distance ship from Norway, called Nordlys or Northern Light, had docked in the harbor of Tallinn. The ship stood at the pier, and the sailors, along with their captain, went ashore to rest and enjoy themselves in the small port city, adorned with typical European stone houses topped with tiled roofs and large medieval streetlamps.

The snow had already melted, but a chill still lingered, and strong, cold winds blew in from the Baltic Sea. Elsa glanced at the horizon that evening as the winds howled, a strange unease settling in her chest. The sea had always been a friend to Tallinn, but lately, it seemed to whisper of storms to come.

Elsa worked in a bar-restaurant, and each evening she dressed and applied her makeup as if she were heading to a romantic rendezvous. On this evening, she wore a flared blue skirt and a white silk blouse tied with a bow. Music played on the gramophone. The patrons drank beer and, occasionally, something stronger. In the center of the hall, couples danced the foxtrot. Girls flirted; young men smiled and winked in delight.

It would be a long time before they again docked in friendly Estonia, with its picturesque shores and prosperous crowd.

Eirik Larsen, a tall, blond man with a sun-kissed face and radiant blue eyes, had served as a captain of Norway's merchant marine for several years. His ship, *Nordlys—Northern Light*, had docked in Tallinn, the capital of Estonia. Before setting sail once more on a long voyage, the sailors wished to spend one last evening enjoying the welcoming city, its stunning shores, and the dense coniferous forests framing the Baltic coastline.

As the captain stood on the deck, twilight fading into night, he inhaled the sharp sea air. There was something heavy about it tonight, something he couldn't quite name. The world was changing —he could feel it in the way countries whispered of war, and ports once bustling with trade now seemed guarded, almost wary. He wondered how much longer such peaceful visits would be possible.

The captain approached the bar counter and asked Elsa to serve him a Scotch with ice. Elsa smiled at the captain and asked, "Where are you from?"

The captain replied,

"I'm from Oslo, Norway. My name is Eirik Larsen. And what's your name?"

The 19-year-old barmaid responded, "Elsa," adding that she lived in Tallinn with her parents, who had once come from Denmark. Again, Elsa gave him an inviting smile.

Elsa was fluent in several languages—Norwegian, Danish, and Estonian.

Captain Larsen immediately extended his hand and suggested, "Let's meet tonight, around nine, right here by the bar. I'll walk you home. It's what we do—where I come from, we always escort our young ladies home if they're out late."

Elsa asked for an early leave, and as soon as she slipped out of the bar, the captain was already waiting outside. He sat on a bench, smoking his pipe. The moment Eirik saw Elsa, he rose, approached her, and took her arm. Together, they began walking down the street. Elsa said nothing. Night had fallen, and the city's lanterns flickered to life, casting their warm glow over the cobbled streets.

As they strolled through the quiet streets, the wind carried the faint sound of distant voices—low, hushed, and secretive. Eirik paused, glancing behind him, but saw nothing unusual. Yet the unease lingered. He forced a smile and tightened his hold on Elsa's arm.

They walked to the park and sat on a bench. The captain told Elsa the steamer would first sail to Norway. "There, we will refuel and rest, and from Oslo, we will sail for a long time—first through the Skagerrak Strait, then across the North Sea into the Atlantic and beyond... It will be a long time before we return home. But when the Nordlys comes back to Norway, I want to go straight to Estonia to see you again, Elsa. I've never met a girl as beautiful as you."

Elsa smiled and said, "That's because my grandmother was from Denmark," nodding in agreement.

Eirik chuckled softly, then grew serious. "It's a strange time, Elsa. The seas feel restless—and so do the nations. My crew and I talk about it sometimes. What if the waters we know so well suddenly become dangerous? What if..." He trailed off, unwilling to voice the thoughts that had haunted him. Instead, he looked at Elsa and added, "But you... you make me forget all of it."

As they parted, the captain embraced her and kissed her deeply. "Well then, farewell. Wait for next spring!"

And so, spring of 1938 arrived, and Elsa and Eirik Larsen met again in Estonia. They married, and a year later, had a son they named Hans. They lived in a cozy apartment in Tallinn. They had enough, and they never worried about the future. They raised their son, loved each other, and rejoiced in life, grateful for that fateful meeting in Tallinn in 1937.

But on November 30, 1939, Soviet troops invaded Finland, and the Winter War began.

The Baltic states froze, uncertain of what lay ahead. Then, in 1940, Soviet forces occupied the Baltics. Stalin sought to seize what many called the Pearl of Europe—the Baltic Sea coast. Lithuania's president fled to Germany, and Soviet troops quickly occupied the remaining territories.

The Baltic peoples, under pressure, voted to join the USSR. Neither Finland, Sweden, nor Denmark could intervene. Soon after, Soviet power expropriated and nationalized private property across the region.

Stalin ordered the deportation of women and children first sending them to the far northern reaches of the USSR, harsh and nearly uninhabitable.

Members of the Soviet government, led by Stalin, spoke over the radio, their voices amplified by loudspeakers set up in major cities. The clipped tone of their declarations carried the weight of finality, as if freedom itself had been snuffed out. Stalin's speeches rang out sharply, his Georgian accent unmistakable. Posters of his heavily retouched, brightly colored image adorned buildings—depicting him as a benevolent patriarch surrounded by rosy-cheeked children, grotesque to those who saw through the thin veneer of propaganda.

Panic began to spread across the Baltic cities. Whispers of mass deportations rippled through the streets—hushed, yet laden with dread. People could not grasp what was truly happening. Soviet tanks rolled in, soldiers barking orders through loudspeakers in Russian, aimed at the local population. Windows shuttered hastily, doors locked tight—but there was no refuge from the gathering storm.

At first light, Elsa and Eirik quietly gathered their most precious and essential belongings. The silence in their home was oppressive, broken only by the rustle of preparations. Everything they owned fit into a single chest. They took a sled, bundled their son warmly, and dressed in layers to brace against the cold. Before sunrise, while the streets were still deserted, they slipped away into the dense coniferous forest beyond Tallinn.

Eirik glanced back once at the fading silhouette of their house. He thought of Hans' first steps, Elsa's laughter echoing off the walls—and felt a pang of despair. But he turned forward. To hesitate was to risk all. They had no destination, only the urgency to flee Soviet control.

Cradled in Elsa's arms, Hans slept soundly. She held him tightly, his cheek against her chest, soothed by the rhythm of her heartbeat. Her thoughts swirled with fear: *Where will we go? Will we survive?* Each step felt like a wager with fate. From time to time, Hans made soft, contented sounds in his sleep.

Eirik pulled the sled, Elsa beside him, child in her arms, whispering silent prayers. By nine o'clock, pale winter sunlight pierced the fog. The light felt indifferent, casting long shadows that mocked their flight. Exhaustion crept in. Hans stirred, then cried. Elsa held him close and sang softly. Her lullaby trembled; comfort laced with a quiet plea for deliverance.

He calmed. Eirik, scanning the tree line, spotted a small house in the distance. Without a word, he made for it.

Perhaps it's abandoned, he thought. The door bore a thick padlock. He tested it. It held. But beside the house was a neat pile of firewood —and a small axe. Taking it up, Eirik struck the handle carefully. The lock clattered to the ground. He paused, heart racing, half-expecting soldiers to emerge from the trees.

Nothing.

He entered. Frost coated the walls, breath rising in the air like smoke. The house was sparse. A long wooden table stood by the window, flanked not by chairs but a bench that wrapped around the room.

They must've fled, Eirik thought. *Or were taken, like so many others.* Their absence haunted the silence. There had been no time for the owners to retrieve their things.

Elsa settled on the sofa, bared her breast, and nursed her son with warm mother's milk. He calmed instantly and drifted into peaceful sleep. Eirik brought in firewood, tossing it onto the floor before lighting a fire. The crackling flames stood defiant—a fragile flicker of warmth against the fear pressing in from all sides. The room began to fill with heat, a small refuge from the harsh world outside.

A few paintings and family photographs hung on the walls. The table bore a long-embroidered runner. In the kitchen beyond, pots and pans hung neatly on the walls. A cupboard held dishes, and beside it stood a small stove with a built-in gas canister.

While Elsa tended to Hans, Eirik searched the shelves. He found jars with screw-top lids filled with tea, cocoa, blackberry jam, and crispbread—the kind common in Norway, Denmark, and Sweden. There were also dried herbs and packets of salted fish. He exhaled in relief. At least they wouldn't starve. But how long could they stay before someone came?

We won't starve, Eirik told himself. *I'll fish while the war rages.*

But he didn't yet know the war was only beginning. After the Soviets, Hitler's forces would come, plunging the region into years of violence—until Germans surrendered on May 8, 1945.

In the deep woods of Võrumaa, where the birches stood like pale sentinels against the snow, Elsa and Eirik found a semblance of shelter from the world's unraveling. Their cabin, little more than a timbered hush between the trees, stood hidden beneath a blanket of white and silence. Here, they weathered the waning fury of war and the hush that followed, living quietly for six long years after the guns fell silent in 1945. But in those early months of that same year, as snow still draped the forest floor and smoke from distant battles curled faintly through the sky, a different cry pierced the hush. Guided by the weatherworn hands of Maarja, the village midwife who had braved the frost and patrols to reach them, Elsa gave birth to their daughter beneath the rafters of their forest haven. Ingrid's first breath steamed in the cold air, her cry rising like a defiant ember against the long night, a sign that even amidst sorrow and silence, life insisted upon its place.

"You mustn't worry," Eirik said gently. "The Scandinavian press will hear of this soon enough. They won't stop you. The Soviets haven't yet chosen successors. God willing, we'll get out of here. Take care of the children—that's all that matters. Here's some money—keep it hidden, even from those you trust. Leave the rest to me. I'm a captain of the high seas, Elsa, but this... this is the greatest storm I've ever faced. I've sailed through raging oceans before—but this is a different kind of peril."

After years under the Soviet heel, Eirik Larsen faced a final test: to slip aboard a Norwegian tanker anchored off the Baltic coast. Under cover of night, he waded through the shallows of the sea, each step a quiet defiance of the invisible chains that had bound him.

Searchlights swept the sky, briefly illuminating the tanker. Remaining unseen by the Soviet coast guard was vital.

He pressed forward, dressed in light, practical clothes: a knitted hat, a loose sweater, and soft boots suited for climbing the rope ladder. But the cold was merciless. His teeth chattered; his limbs were numb. Still, the image of Elsa and the children waiting for him burned in his mind.

Failure was unthinkable.

In the stillness, he heard the waves striking the tanker's hull—familiar, almost comforting. Norwegian voices rang out across the water, mingling with the sound of the sea. It was the voice of home —and with it, the promise of freedom.

It felt like an eternity as he waded through the water, battling its resistance with every step, when at last, he saw a light ahead.

Norwegian sailors in a small boat had spotted him and were signaling.

Spurred by the sight of the lifeboat bearing Norwegian emblems, Eirik pushed through exhaustion and cold. When he reached it, the sailors hauled him aboard without a word. The boat glided swiftly toward the Norwegian tanker anchored in Estonian coastal waters.

As they neared the ship, a rope ladder was lowered from above. A crewman leaned over the railing, shouting:

"Grab the rails! Climb up! Don't look down!"

Eirik's hands trembled from cold and strain as he gripped the rope ladder. The climb felt endless. Each step was agony; his arms screamed in protest. He whispered a prayer and focused on the rhythm—hand, foot, hand. At last, the deck appeared. With a final surge, he hoisted himself over the railing and collapsed.

Gasping, he barely noticed the man approaching until he heard, "Captain Larsen." It was Captain Karl Magnussen. He saluted. For a moment, Eirik couldn't respond. His chest heaved. Tears froze on his cheeks. Then, with a trembling hand, he returned the salute.

He was among his countrymen again. Strength returned.

The crew gathered, their faces a mix of curiosity and awe. They didn't yet know the full story, but they knew he had fled the Soviet Union. They threw a blanket over his soaked shoulders. The ship's cook handed him water and a sandwich, which he devoured in silence.

In a private cabin, still shivering, Eirik pulled out his tattered Norwegian passport and credentials from his days aboard the Nord Lys. The papers were creased and worn. The photograph inside showed a younger man—his own face, but from another life. He stared at it, barely able to reconcile the two versions of himself.

This was his key to freedom. Captain Magnussen studied the documents, then looked at Eirik's face and nodded silently.

Once Eirik had calmed, he recounted his tale—how he had met two Norwegian sailors near the docks the day before his planned escape and how they had given him hope. The crew listened intently as he described his perilous journey through the icy shallows, unseen and unheard, carried forward only by faith, his mother tongue, and the determination to survive.

At midnight, the Norwegian tanker departed without signal or sound, slipping silently into darkness. It sailed through the Skagerrak Strait, then across the North Sea, toward the welcoming shores of Norway, shrouded in dense forests and majestic fjords. Eirik stood on the deck, watching the horizon unfold into the promise of freedom. The salt spray mingled with his tears, and for the first time in years, he allowed himself a flicker of hope.

The captain of the tanker sent a telegram from aboard, reporting they had taken on former captain Eirik Larsen, who had escaped from Estonia, one of the Baltic republics under Soviet control.

As the ship neared Norwegian shores and dropped anchor, Eirik was awaited by the local coast guard. They placed him in a car and brought him to the municipal offices in Oslo. There, he was met by representatives of Norway's secret services. For several hours, Eirik was interrogated, the details of his escape held in strictest secrecy.

The agents questioned him meticulously, their faces impassive, eyes watchful. Eirik sensed that any inconsistency might shatter his fragile hope. But he spoke calmly, recounting each harrowing moment with the precision of a captain navigating treacherous waters.

First, his Norwegian documents—those tattered papers presented aboard the ship—were examined. Then, his biography was verified, cross-referenced against his testimony. Every crease, every worn edge of his passport seemed to whisper the years of exile.

Eirik's first day in Oslo stretched into evening. The interrogation room, with sterile lighting and impersonal walls, felt a world away from the comfort of his ship's cabin. After exhausting hours of questioning, he was taken to a seafood restaurant. The aroma of grilled salmon and steaming potatoes brought back memories of the life he had lost. Each bite felt like reclaiming a piece of himself.

That night, in a hotel room provided by the agency, he collapsed onto the sofa and fell into a deep sleep. In his dreams, Elsa, Hans, and Ingrid smiled at him, and he whispered, "Hold on, my love. We will all be together soon. I promise."

The interrogations continued daily, though conducted with respect and growing trust. The officials knew how nearly impossible it was to escape the USSR during those years. Still, the shadow of the Cold War loomed, and caution prevailed.

Norway's security services had to be certain. Was Larsen a true escapee—or a Soviet plant? "Trust is earned, not given lightly," one agent said, studying Eirik. "These are dangerous times, Captain." But after a thorough investigation, they concluded his escape was genuine—a daring and extraordinary success. His calm under pressure, the intricate details, and the scars on his hands told the story for him.

It was 1953, the height of the Cold War, a time of deep mistrust between the Soviet Union and the nations of Western Europe and America. In the dimly lit offices of Norway's intelligence headquarters, whispers of spies and defections colored every interaction with uncertainty.

A week after his questioning concluded, Norway's social services issued Eirik Larsen new identification documents to replace his expired passport. Holding them in his hands, he felt a surge of bittersweet emotion—freedom, at last, but incomplete without Elsa and the children. He was given an apartment in the city center and offered help in finding work.

Having lived behind the Iron Curtain during one of the USSR's darkest periods, Eirik had become fluent in Russian. His unique background and language skills soon led to an invitation to work for Norway's national security services.

"You've navigated treacherous waters, Captain Larsen," a senior official told him. "Now help us navigate ours."

The position was well-paid, and Eirik began to think in earnest about rescuing Elsa and the children from the USSR. Each passing day deepened his resolve, though uncertainty weighed on every decision.

One day, Mr. Oliver Johansen, an attorney and a representative of Norway's security service, met with Eirik—not in an office, but in a quiet city café. The aroma of freshly ground coffee and warm pastries stood in stark contrast to the steel and suspicion of his earlier debriefings.

By then, Eirik's appearance had changed. He was clean-shaven, his hair neatly trimmed. Though streaked with silver, it gave him a distinguished air. He looked strong and upright, with the bearing of a man shaped by the sea. His transformation was symbolic—no longer a shadow of Soviet oppression, but a captain restored to dignity. His blue eyes gleamed once more with a light long dimmed. As he sat at the café table, he reflected again on his escape, which had come at the perfect moment—just after Stalin's death.

For years, Eirik had followed news from the West. When Stalin's passing sent ripples through the Soviet hierarchy, he recognized a fleeting moment of change—a crack in the Iron Curtain he had long awaited. He seized it. "Sometimes even iron crumbles," he had said. "And when it does, you must be ready."

As he recounted his story to Norway's intelligence officials, Eirik emphasized his years of vigilance. He knew no ordinary escape was possible from behind the Curtain. Yet, somehow, the chance had come. "It wasn't just luck," he said. "It was vigilance, timing, and faith that freedom would call when I was ready to answer."

"God was on my side," he often added, though he credited practicalities too—especially his fluency in Norwegian, a language rarely spoken beyond Scandinavia. In Norway, even small communities spoke several languages, and all documentation was maintained in both Norwegian and English.

During his escape, Eirik's most valuable possessions had been his worn Norwegian passport and naval credentials. These, along with his merchant and fishing licenses, had granted him credibility. Now, they symbolized not just survival—but the future he was determined to reclaim for his family.

About a month after commencing his new role, Eirik was summoned to a building housing the ministry overseeing Norway's security. The structure's stark modern design and guarded entrances resembled a fortress amidst the Cold War's chaos. Here, Eirik's plans would advance significantly.

At the ministry, Eirik was greeted by Oliver Johansen, who extended his hand with a familiar warmth.

"We spoke not long ago," Johansen said with a slight smile. "At the café—about life, and everything beyond it."

He continued, his tone firm yet encouraging: "I've considered your situation, Captain Larsen. In coordination with the Ministry of Internal Affairs, I've decided to act as your representative in the

USSR. We'll officially register your marriage to Elsa at the Tallinn municipal office. I'll personally deliver Norwegian passports for Elsa, listing your children's names. Once registered, Elsa and your children will gain significant legal protection.

"Regardless of Soviet actions, the KGB's hands will be tied. Your family will fall under Norwegian law's full protection."

Eirik listened intently, his heart pounding as he envisioned Elsa, Hans, and Ingrid. Images of Elsa's weary yet strong face and his children's innocent smiles flooded his mind. He nodded in agreement, praying silently for their safety.

Johansen leaned forward, his voice steady: "This won't be simple. We know the USSR operates on 'blat'—connections and favors. We'll do the same, bringing substantial gifts to smooth the process. Given their location in the Baltic region, local resentment toward Soviet occupiers may aid us."

After a pause, Johansen added, "I propose sending a Lutheran priest to Elsa with your message and necessary funds. The Lutheran and Catholic churches maintain connections in the Baltic region and can facilitate this delivery."

Reflectively, Johansen posed a pressing question: "Should we register the marriage officially or arrange an escape? A fishing schooner could transport us across the Baltic Sea to a safe harbor—perhaps Hamburg."

Eirik tensed, overwhelmed by emotion. He couldn't speak, but his silent nod conveyed resolute agreement. His mind raced: register the marriage or risk a daring escape? Each option bore immense risks, but he was determined to bring Elsa and the children to safety.

As the meeting concluded, Johansen stood, speaking with quiet resolve: "Consider our course carefully, Captain Larsen. You understand life in Soviet-ruled Estonia better than anyone. Your insight will guide our decision."

They shook hands firmly, a gesture of unspoken trust and determination. Parting ways, each man was consumed by plans and hopes. For Eirik, the café's warmth vanished as he stepped into the Norwegian chill, mirroring the enormity of the task ahead.

Meanwhile, Elsa continued her life of quiet resilience in the village, holding onto faith in a future that seemed impossibly distant.

She waited and believed that someone would come to them, bringing a letter from Eirik. But a month passed, then another, and so many months slipped by. Still, Elsa waited for news from her husband.

Each morning, she rose very early, prepared for the day, and walked to the local market to sell vegetables and strawberries that she grew on a small patch of fertile soil. She carried heavy bags filled with fresh produce from her garden and hard-boiled eggs laid by their two hens. In a separate large basket were pies stuffed with cabbage and potatoes, which she had baked in the early morning.

Her days were a routine of labor and quiet hope. Each pie she baked, every step she took to the market, was a prayer for Eirik's safe return. Yet as the seasons changed, doubt began to creep into her heart like the cold Baltic winds that whistled through the forest.

Hans and Ingrid attended the local school together. They were never late, even in bad weather. Through heavy rain and snowstorms, they walked three kilometers through the forest to school and back again.

When the children returned home, Elsa would immediately place before them a large plate of hearty vegetable soup and a piece of dark rye bread, which she baked herself. On Sundays, they would have a roasted chicken leg cooked over the fire. After lunch, the children read books and went to bed early, by nine o'clock. No one asked questions. They all waited for a miracle—a letter from Eirik Larsen.

Then, on one stormy autumn day, there came a knock at the door.

The sound startled Elsa, cutting through the relentless pounding of rain against the windows. Her heart raced as she wiped her hands on her apron and hurried to the door.

Elsa rushed to answer it, not even asking who it was before opening the door to the hallway. Standing before her was a tall man in a rain-soaked coat. He was utterly drenched, his lips barely moving as he tried to speak.

Perhaps he's frozen, Elsa thought. She gestured with her hand, inviting the stranger to remove his coat, and at last, the man spoke in Norwegian:

"I am from Eirik Larsen. My name is Father Thomas. I come from the Lutheran Church."

The room seemed to hold its breath. Elsa's hand gripped the edge of the door, her mind spinning as she processed his words. This was the moment she had prayed for, but it felt like a dream.

Elsa fell silent, her body tensing. That day, the village had been celebrating some pagan festival, but Elsa had not gone to the market because of the heavy rain. The children had stayed home as well.

Father Thomas took a burlap bag filled with supplies, set the bundles down on the table, and said, "This is for you, Elsa."

He hesitated, cleared his throat, and continued, "Your husband, Eirik Larsen, is in Norway, in the city of Oslo. He has found work and now has a two-room apartment in the center of the city."

Then Father Thomas took out a small stack of money and placed it on the table.

"This is to help you," he said.

"Now, let us have something to eat and talk," he added, as Elsa began unwrapping the supplies he had brought. The children sat silently at the table, patiently waiting while Elsa arranged the food on small plates. For the first time, they saw smoked sausage, a wedge of Danish cheese, Swiss chocolate bars, and even crispbread. There were tea bags, ground coffee, and a box of chocolates as well.

The sight of such luxuries brought tears to Elsa's eyes. For so long, they had lived on the edge of survival, and this moment felt like a glimpse of a better world—a world Eirik had promised them.

Father Thomas pulled out a small bottle of cognac, pouring a little into a glass to warm himself. From his seemingly endless bag, he retrieved warm knitted scarves and hats for Elsa, Ingrid, and Hans. Finally, he placed a letter on the table, written in beautiful Norwegian script.

Elsa took the letter, her hands trembling, tears rolling down her cheeks as she brushed them away.

My dearest Elsa,

Every night I see your face in my dreams, and every dawn I rise with one purpose—to bring you home. I've not forgotten a single thing: the way you smiled beneath the birch trees, the songs you sang to the children, the warmth of your hands in mine. Hold fast. Spring will come, and with it—freedom.

Yours until the last tide,

Eirik

As Elsa read Eirik's letter, tears streamed down her cheeks. She clutched the paper to her chest, as if it were a lifeline. Hans and

Ingrid sat silently, their eyes fixed on their mother, sensing the gravity of the moment.

Father Thomas, a slender man with silver hair and kind blue eyes, spoke softly in fluent Norwegian. His presence, though unexpected, brought a sense of calm. Elsa listened intently, nodding occasionally.

The priest, likely granted a special visa under the Soviet Union's allowance for religious aid missions in the Baltic states, had managed to reach them despite the KGB's vigilant oversight of foreign visitors.

Given the relentless storm outside—rain mixed with hail and wind bending the trees—Elsa invited Father Thomas to stay the night. He accepted gratefully.

She prepared the guest room, a modest space with a sofa and a radio capable of picking up broadcasts from the West. After drinking a glass of milk, Father Thomas retired for the night. Elsa, placing Eirik's letter under her pillow, joined her children in their room. As sleep overtook her, memories of her first meeting with Eirik in Tallinn filled her dreams, bringing a smile to her face.

The next morning, a brief respite in the weather allowed sunlight to pierce the clouds, but it was fleeting. Gray skies soon returned, mirroring Elsa's mix of hope and apprehension.

Dressed in a black cassock and warm sweater, Father Thomas prepared to depart. "Our Lord willing, we will meet in Oslo this spring," he said, accepting a letter Elsa had written for Eirik, which he tucked into a hidden pocket of his coat.

He stepped into the damp forest, the earthy scent of mushrooms and pine needles in the air, leaning on a walking stick Elsa had provided.

Beyond their quiet village, the Soviet Union was undergoing significant upheaval. In 1953, Lavrentiy Beria, once Stalin's close associate, was arrested and executed for treason. Georgy Malenkov briefly assumed leadership, followed by Nikolai Bulganin. By 1955, Nikita Khrushchev had consolidated power.

That same winter, word began to stir across the Soviet bloc—a secret speech, whispered through embassies and smuggled past borders. Khrushchev had dared to denounce Stalin, lifting a corner of the dark curtain. Somehow, the words reached the West, and soon the world knew. For the first time in years, something began to shift —just a little, like ice cracking beneath the sun.

The following early spring, Oliver Johansen—now central to Eirik Larsen's plan—traveled to Estonia under diplomatic cover. His stated mission: to aid the Baltic region by reconnecting families separated by war. But the true task was far more dangerous—a race against Soviet suspicion.

Instead of flying to Moscow, Johansen boarded a Baltic excursion ship that made a stop in Estonia for refueling. By avoiding Moscow, he sidestepped the KGB's scrutiny, which typically shadowed all foreign arrivals in the Soviet capital. He planned to enter the Baltics from Europe, circumventing Soviet central control.

Upon arriving in Tallinn, Johansen was struck by its European charm —grocery stores stocked with fine dairy and fresh breads, streets full of people in modest but respectable attire.

He spent the night at a local hotel. Though he spoke Russian, his strong accent posed a risk. A single misstep could spark suspicion. Still, his resolve held firm.

Early the next morning, he checked out and walked toward the train station, stopping at a shop to buy a plain pair of trousers and a sweater. In the fitting room, he changed, adopting the look of a local.

He purchased a one-way ticket to a coastal town surrounded by remote beaches and dense forest. Upon arrival, a quick glance at his map told him he'd need to trek several kilometers through the woods to reach Elsa's cottage.

The half-moon gave way to the morning sun, quickly swallowed by a drifting mist. Though spring had arrived, the air remained brisk, the Baltic wind laced with salt. The forest smelled of mushrooms, wild strawberries, and pine.

As he walked, Johansen ran over contingency plans. He carried diplomatic credentials and gifts to smooth his path, but even these might not save him if the Soviets grew suspicious. Every rustle in the underbrush set his nerves on edge.

At one point, he passed a forager gathering honey mushrooms. The man, unfazed by the stranger, greeted him in Russian: "Privet," a casual hello.

Johansen gave a curt nod and moved on.

Eventually, he found the house Elsa had described. In the garden, he spotted her—head scarfed, weeding rows of plants.

Approaching her, he said simpler: "Oliver Johansen." The words hung in the air, bridging two worlds. Elsa understood immediately and smiled. She invited him inside. "It's more comfortable to talk indoors," she said.

Oliver spoke fluent Norwegian and passable Russian, though with a thick accent.

Inside, he handed Hans and Ingrid bundles of clothing. "Put these on. We'll take the train to Tallinn and register your mother's marriage. Don't worry, Hans—this is how we'll get you all aboard a merchant or excursion ship departing from the port."

He then gave Elsa a large bag. Inside was a white dress with a delicate floral pattern and a pair of leather shoes with thin heels.

"Please change now," Oliver said urgently. "We have little time and no help. Everything must be done today."

When Elsa stepped out, she wore the new dress, her golden hair loose in soft waves. Hans was in a white shirt and new shoes, and Ingrid had on a colorful dress, patent shoes, and white socks.

Oliver addressed them warmly: "Now we are ready. Remember—we're registering the marriage to invoke international protections. After that, we'll convince customs to let us board a ship. Our goal is to finalize the marriage in a Lutheran church in Norway."

His voice was calm, but his eyes betrayed the tension of a man gambling with fate.

"I insist on this plan," he said firmly. "I believe I can persuade them. I have gifts."

"In this country, marrying a foreigner means applying for approval —a six-month process. After registration, you must request exit permits, which could take even longer. We must bypass all of it."

"That's why," he said, turning to Elsa, "we'll register the marriage under exceptional grounds—especially since you are expecting a child. This certificate may be vital if Soviet authorities stop us. So, we must risk it—and aim to board a merchant ship or even a fishing schooner."

The weight of his words settled over the room. Elsa looked at her children, then at Oliver, and nodded. There was no turning back. Radio reports soon confirmed the presence of a foreign fishing vessel anchored in the Baltic Sea. Oliver saw a narrow window of opportunity—and knew it might be their last.

As twilight fell, he led Elsa and the children through the empty streets toward the pier. A brisk wind blew off the Baltic. The small fishing boat, marked with foreign emblems, sat anchored offshore—a fragile promise.

If it had been only him and Elsa, he might have swum for it. But with the children, such risk was unthinkable. Scanning the shoreline, he saw the pier was empty. A shift change in the 'militia' patrol left a brief opening. Oliver's pulse quickened, but his resolve was firm.

He raised a Norwegian flag and signaled the schooner for assistance. The fishermen responded, jumping into a lifeboat and rowing to shore.

Above, the stars glittered, but danger crept closer. Border patrol searchlights sliced through the darkness like accusing fingers. Every second dragged. Every noise echoed with dread. If caught, they could all be executed as defectors.

And yet—perhaps due to the chaos of the post-Stalin era, perhaps because they were on the more lenient shores of Estonia—fate held its breath.

No one dared breathe as the sailors in the small inflatable boat approached the shore. Their movements were efficient but tense, as though they, too, understood the gravity of the moment. One by one, they lifted everyone aboard—first the children, then Elsa, and finally, Oliver Johansen.

Oliver climbed into the boat himself, taking up one of the oars to help row. The freezing water soaked his boots, and the salty spray stung his face, but adrenaline kept him going. After about twenty minutes, they reached the Danish fishing vessel anchored nearby. One by one, they were lifted aboard via a hoist.

Once safely on deck, Elsa and the children burst into tears, overwhelmed with emotion. The release of tension was palpable, mingling with sheer exhaustion. Captain Hans Andersen emerged and saluted Oliver, who, smiling through his own tears, returned the gesture and declared:

"I, Oliver Johansen, diplomat of the Kingdom of Norway, have safely accompanied Elsa—a Danish national—and her two children, Hans and Ingrid, from Soviet-occupied Estonia. We are presently en route to Hamburg aboard your vessel, where she is to be reunited with her husband, Eirik Larsen, who fled the Soviet Union in the months following Stalin's death. I respectfully request that this message be transmitted by telegraph."

His voice was steady, though his eyes shone with a mix of triumph and fatigue. He repeated the statement for clarity, then added, "My deepest thanks for granting us passage."

Captain Andersen descended to the cabin and returned with warm clothes, water, and sandwiches. Within minutes, the ship set sail. The low hum of the engine echoed like a heartbeat in the night. As darkness fell, they moved silently into the Baltic Sea, avoiding radar detection.

The cold wind cut through their borrowed clothes, and the ship's sway wore on aching muscles. Yet no one complained. They huddled close, the children clutching Elsa, who stared out at the shoreline. Salty spray soaked them, and Elsa silently bid farewell to Estonia— its golden beaches, pine forests, and the life she once knew.

Guided by the full moon, the schooner pressed on toward Germany.

By early morning, the port city of Hamburg appeared on the horizon. The bustling harbor was almost surreal—a bright contrast to the fear they'd left behind.

Elsa and the children stood on deck, gripping the railing. Nearby, Oliver Johansen watched the familiar port he had visited many times, both for work and leisure.

The air buzzed with the sounds of life—ships docking, gulls crying, engines droning. Colorful banners fluttered, and the wet cobblestones shimmered under the sun. Beyond the harbor rose tall buildings, shops, and restaurants bustling with morning activity.

Elsa could hardly believe she was so close to reuniting with Eirik, whom she hadn't seen in two years. Hans had grown tall—now the same height as Oliver—and looked strikingly like his father, with bright blue eyes and sun-lightened hair. Ingrid, with her wavy caramel hair and gray-blue eyes, was the image of her mother.

The schooner, marked as part of a joint Danish Norwegian company, eased toward the pier and dropped anchor. A rope ladder was lowered. Elsa, accompanied by the captain, descended first. Hans, Ingrid, and Oliver followed.

Waiting on the pier was Eirik Larsen, surrounded by journalists. In his hands was a bouquet of colorful balloons swaying in the breeze.

As soon as Elsa saw him, she ran, and Eirik ran to meet her. They embraced tightly, clinging to one another without words. For a moment, the world faded. Tears streamed down Elsa's face as cameras clicked, capturing the reunion.

Hans and Ingrid joined them, and Eirik embraced and kissed them both. Hans, now his father's height, looked thin but strong. Ingrid, delicate and quiet, stood like a mirror of Elsa's youth.

A newspaper reporter guided them to a gold-beige Mercedes waiting nearby. The family moved together—laughter and tears interwoven —a fragile, triumphant testament to their journey.

"We'll fly to Norway soon," Eirik said, his voice tight with emotion. "Until we find our own home, we'll stay in my apartment in Oslo."

Elsa clutched his arm, whispering to herself, "This isn't a dream—it's real."

In the years to come, their story would be told and retold—a whispered legend of courage carried across sea and silence. In quiet moments, Elsa would look out the window of their home in Oslo, the children grown, Eirik's hand in hers, and remember the forest paths, the salted spray, and the prayers spoken under breath. They had survived the storm not by strength alone, but by love, loyalty, and the stubborn hope that freedom still waited on the far side of fear. And so, it was—not history, but devotion—that finally brought them home.

Table of Contents

NORTHERN CODE

(Untitled)   101